LARRY D. BLACK

NEVER
Give Up

Scroggins Family Series No.12

NEVER GIVE UP
Copyright © 2022 Larry D. Black

All intellectual property rights are reserved. Except for brief quotations incorporated in critical articles and reviews, no part of this book may be used or reproduced by any means, graphic, electronic, or mechanical, including photocopying, recording, taping, or information storage and retrieval system, without the written permission of the author.

Media Literary Excellence
508 West 26th Street, Kearney, NE 68848
www.medialiteraryexcellence.com
1-402-819-3224

Because of the dynamic nature of the Internet, any web addresses or URLs can be changed at any time. Links in this book may have changed since it was first published, and it's possible that it's no longer valid. The opinions stated in the work are strictly those of the author. The views expressed here are those of the author and do not necessarily reflect those of the publisher. The publisher expressly disclaims any and all liability for them.

Any individuals represented in stock imagery given by copyright-free sites are the property of their respective owners. The usage of models and similar images is solely for illustrative purposes.

ISBN (Paperback): 978-1-958082-00-3
ISBN (Ebook): 978-1-958082-01-0

Printed in the United States of America

Foreword

Never Give Up is another book about the Scroggins Family and like the previous writings, this book is completely fictional and any use of any actual names and/or events is strictly coincidental.

This story is about Richard Scroggins who is a football recruiting scout for the LSU Tigers. Upon discovering an exceptional talent, the attempt to get him signed for the Tigers became a drama that led to never imaginable consequences.

This book has enough drama, romance, adventure, and compassion that it should appeal to all readers. As with the previous novels, you are made to feel a part of the Scroggins Family as if they were your own family.

I hope you enjoy reading the story as much as I did writing it.

~ Larry

Characters within the Book.

Richard Scroggins – main character
Logan (Allen Beaullieu) Pointe – football star
Willy & Loretta Constant – Logan's caregiver
Bob Williams – Logan's football coach
Talisa – girl at Clearwater café
Robert Hagan – Hopes Landing sheriff
Coach Bevels – LSU head football coach
Roger and Tieo Beaullieu - Logan's father and mother
Enola and Dee Beaullieu - Logan's sisters
Allen Beaullieu – Logan's real name
Mr. Sanders – Hopes Landing school superintendent
Mike Hopkins – Hopes Landing athletic director
Dr. Stinson – Angelina County Hospital doctor
Robert and Janet Scroggins– Richard's Dad and Stepmom
Paige, Tiffany, and Darrin - Janet's children
     (Richard's step brother & sisters)
Rachael – Richard's sister
Taylor – young FBI agent
Roscoe – Cajun fisherman
Pepe and Alex – Roscoe's sons
Albert Jennings – FBI agent friend of Richard's dad

Betsy – FBI contact in Idaho
Albert Kinsley – chief FBI agent in Idaho
Cap-a-tan Lopez –head of Idaho compound
Lawson Davis – Ski Lodge Manager

1
Chapter

It was a beautiful crisp fall Friday morning and after parking my car in the designated area, I walked into the building and made my way over to the register, and signed my name, Richard Scroggins. The last time I was in this funeral home was for the service of my mother who was killed quite a few years ago. I was at least an hour early for the service, and I was amazed at how many people were already here. Some of them were mingling and visiting, and I could hear an occasional ring of laughter. Others were in the chapel sitting quietly and reverently and presumably remembering the life of Ben Scroggins. Some were reading the obituary that was handed to them as they entered the building and signed the guest register. It was very apparent that Uncle Ben was a very popular and well-respected man. Although most of his generation had already stepped into eternity, the generations after him were the ones who were here to pay their final respects.

After signing the guest register, I made my way down the hall to where the family had gathered and was quickly met by my cousin, Toby, from Alaska. He slapped me on the back and said, "Hey, Richard! I'm glad you were able to make it. You sure look good. It appears life has been treating you well."

"Yeah, things have been running pretty smoothly. How are you doing? It's been too long since we've seen each other! You're looking pretty good yourself. Have you seen Janet and Dad?" He pointed to where they were, and I eased over that way. When they saw me, they stopped their conversation and held out their arms to embrace me. It was so good to see them as it had been a long time since I had been home. At this time of the year, I was pretty involved with my career as a recruiting scout for the LSU Tigers football team.

The hour passed quickly as I was visiting with many of my family members that I hadn't seen in several years. I made my way over to Aunt Mary Ann. I told her that I used to love going to their house on Thanksgiving, and part of the reason was to hear Uncle Ben tell stories from the past. He made them seem so real and gave me a sense of pride in my heritage. She smiled and said she had heard the same sentiments from at least ten people today. "Ben did have a way of making a story come alive," she said as she wiped her eyes.

Finally, we were escorted into the chapel and seated together as a family when it was time for the service to begin. Several appropriate songs were sung before a few words were given by my Grandpa Pete who was Uncle Ben's baby brother. He spoke of how Uncle Ben had stepped up and become the father figure in their family after their papa had died. "No one asked him to do so - he just did. He was that kind of a man. Whenever there was a need that he could satisfy, he stepped up and did it. Whenever I needed help or advice, I knew I could go to my big brother Ben, and that he would shoot straight with me. And after talking with him, things always looked a little brighter, and I felt much better. There was a time when I couldn't walk because of polio, and Ben and Mary Ann were there, along with Mama and Papa, to encourage me. As we got older, I didn't call on him as much for advice but I still had admiration and respect for the insight and godly wisdom that he had. The world is a brighter place because of my big brother, and I am going to miss him."

Then, one of the county commissioners gave a brief testimony about the impact for good that Uncle Ben had on this part of East Texas - not only as a model citizen but also as a public servant for some twenty-six years as county sheriff. "During his time in office, everyone was treated fairly and justly. It was a dark day in the lives of many of us when he announced that he was resigning his position as sheriff because of his failing health. We all knew that it would be hard, if not impossible, to find a comparable replacement for him," the commissioner said.

Uncle Lewis followed the commissioner and gave the eulogy. He said that as a chaplain, he had been asked to conduct many funerals, but he was more honored to do this one than any other that he had done. He also told some stories of their early boyhood days and emphasized that even at a very young age, Ben felt the responsibility of loyalty. He said that family loyalty influenced his decision to join the army so he could help their papa financially and thus save the family farm. He told about him being a prisoner of war for many years and how all the family presumed he was dead. I was surprised to hear that as I had never heard Uncle Ben mention it. He said Uncle Ben had agonized over whether to run for county sheriff because he feared he was not qualified for the job. However, his loyalty to the community persuaded him to accept the position, and he did an outstanding job for so many years.

Uncle Lewis said loyalty to the community also influenced Uncle Ben's decision to build and manage the orphanage that has served so many needy children. He pointed out a section where people were sitting in the front left of the chapel. This section was filled with middle-aged people as well as younger ones. He said some thirty families, who were Uncle Ben's extended family, were seated there and that they were children, plus families of children, who were once residents of the orphanage. "He loved and nurtured those children as if they were his own. Obviously, they loved him too because so many have come today to pay their final respects. As you can all clearly see, my brother, Ben Scroggins, was a man of influence who made a positive difference in the lives of so many."

Then Uncle Lewis acknowledged another section that was filled with law enforcement officers from every branch. All of them were dressed in their respective uniforms, and it was a real tribute to a man who gave so much of himself to maintain peace, law, and order, and thus made our community a better place to live.

Uncle Lewis closed his part of the service by mentioning Uncle Ben's love for his wife of many years and how their love was indeed a love forever. "'Ben and Mary Ann were two words that seemed to flow as one word because they were unified as one. I know of no one who was more loyal and faithful to his wife than was my brother, Ben, to Mary Ann. He loved her more than life itself. And I know of no one who was more devoted and supportive of a husband than Mary Ann." There was not a dry eye in the house when Uncle Lewis looked at Aunt Mary Ann and said, "You and Ben both honored your vows of long ago to love and cherish and hold one another until death parted you."

Uncle Lewis ended the service by saying, "The family has agreed to inscribe the words, *He made a difference* on the back of Ben Scroggins' headstone." As the service ended, all the family gathered at the orphanage for a family meal and visiting. As you might expect, every small group that was huddled together was telling some story about Uncle Ben. It was getting late. I needed to go because, in a few hours, I needed to be in Center, Texas, to look at a defensive lineman. It was hard for me to say goodbye to everyone, and especially to Janet and Dad. I hoped I would be able to visit them more frequently as life is short and no one can take the place of family.

As I drove toward Center, I thought about the impact Uncle Ben had on the lives of so many people. I wondered if, when I die, people will remember me as a person who made a positive difference in the lives of others. In reality, my career choice gives me the potential to change lives as I make available to many young men the opportunity for an education and possibly a professional career in the NFL (National Football League).

The time passed quickly, and I was soon in the press box waiting for the football game to begin. As far as I knew, I was the only college scout at the game. Center was not having a very good season and thus had not attracted the attention of the press. We had received a tip about a lineman named Casey Carrie. The attraction to him was his size. He was 6' 3" and weighed 315 pounds. If he had any kind of agility at all, we would like for him to consider attending our school. Center was playing Clearwater, a school in the Lake Charles ISD.

I thought it was unusual for a Texas school to be playing a southern Louisiana school. Clearwater really hadn't made much of a name for itself either, so I figured I was in for a boring night. I watched Carrie during the warm-up drills, and he seemed to be coordinated. I jotted down a few notes and took advantage of the complementary hotdogs that the concession stand made available to the press box before the kick-off.

Finally, the game was underway, and I was immediately impressed. However, the boy who caught my eye was not Casey Carrie, but rather it was the running back for the Clearwater Trojans. From the program, I learned that his name was Logan Pointer. He was 6' 1" and weighed 195 pounds, and he was as quick as any back I had ever seen. A couple of times he broke to the sidelines and ran like the wind. There were times when he was in the grasp of several defensive players, but they couldn't get him down. I filled several pages with notes about this young man. I couldn't believe that he hadn't made the sports headlines.

Carrie also had some good qualities. He played well and was certainly a candidate that we might want to pursue, but he didn't make my head spin like the Pointer kid did.

After the game, I was on the cell phone with the coaching staff at LSU and asked if they had any information about Logan Pointer. They had never heard of him. I told them what I observed and they wanted me to talk with both Casey Carrie and Logan Pointer before returning to Baton Rouge.

The next morning, I went to the school at Center and visited with their athletic director who was also their head football coach.

I told him who I was and that I was interested in talking with Casey Carrie about possibly playing for LSU. He seemed delighted by my interest and began to tell me all the good qualities about Casey. I asked about his grades, and he said they were mostly A's with a couple of B's. Academically, he was in the top five percent of his graduating class.

I asked the coach if he would go with me after school to visit Casey and his parents. He called to ask them if we might come, and they were very pleased to have us do so. The Carries lived in what appeared to be the wealthy part of town. I figured their house was in the half-million-dollar range, if not more. A red corvette, which I assumed was Casey's, was parked in the drive. I asked the coach, and he said it did belong to Casey. So I was expecting to be greeted by someone with a high-society, arrogant, and probably rude attitude - but I was wrong.

Casey was an only child, but he was very polite and well-mannered. His parents made me feel very welcome, and I felt that I was an honored guest in their home. Before I left, I thought of them as "salt-of-the-earth" type people.

I told Casey that we had an interest in him playing colligate football for LSU. I tried to impress upon him that he would certainly help our offensive or defensive line, and I invited him and his family to visit our campus and look at our program. Knowing that there would be other schools after him, I wanted him to promise that he would at least visit us before making a commitment agreement. He said that Texas A&M and Baylor had already visited with him, but he promised to give us a look, and I agreed to get back in touch with him as soon as their football season was completed.

I felt good as I left because he agreed to go look at LSU. When he had a chance to visit with our coaching staff and look over the campus, I felt our odds were pretty good at getting him to sign a letter of intent.

The next morning, I headed out to Clearwater, which was not far from the Calcasieu River and some fifteen to twenty miles northeast of Lake Charles. I got to Clearwater a little before noon and decided I'd stop at a local seafood café for a bowl of Louisiana Shrimp Gumbo. I figured from the looks of the place that they would have good gumbo, and I was not disappointed. It was spicy hot - just the way I liked it, and their coffee was extra strong. I got directions to the school from a cute blue-eyed waitress. I noticed that she wasn't wearing a wedding ring, and for some reason, which was unlike me, I asked her if she had any plans for tonight. She said her evening was free, and I asked her if we might get together someplace so we could visit. She said I could pick her up here at the café. We agreed at 7:00 PM and then I left with a song in my heart. It was totally unlike me to be so impulsive, but for some reason, I felt the need to see her again. And I didn't even know her name!

As was my pattern, I went to the athletic department of the school and talked with the director. I introduced myself to Bob Williams and told him that I was an LSU recruiting agent and was interested in talking to Logan Pointer. Immediately, I sensed that something was wrong. Coach Williams began to tell me that Logan was a problem and that he was emotionally unstable. He said that he was in a foster care arrangement and refused to talk about his real parents. "But, the boy can run the football," the coach added.

I told him that I could vouch for that as I saw him in the game against Center. He ran for over one-hundred-fifty yards. "How are his grades?" I asked.

"Terrible. He should not be eligible to play ball, but since he is so good, the administration sorta looks the other way as he squeaks by with D's. Don't misunderstand me. He's not dumb, but he is just a very troubled child and does not apply himself to learning."

"Do you know what's bothering him?"

"No, not for sure as he will not talk about it, but I feel it is all wrapped up with family problems back home."

"Do you think he will talk with me?" I asked.

"Won't know until ya try. Maybe he will if the conversation stays on football."

Coach Williams and I talked for a while, and we both agreed that it might be best if I made the home visit alone. He said he would drive me to the house where he was living. But after introducing me, he would leave and let us talk alone.

I was sure glad he agreed to show me where they lived because it was on a heavily wooded country road with three or four different turns. Finally, we drove up in front of an old, dilapidated-looking house, and my immediate thought was, "Surely this is not where he lives!" But it was. There were several junk cars around and at least six dogs barking.

As we pulled into what appeared to be a driveway, I was expecting some kind of shotgun welcome. But instead, a middle- aged man, with what looked to be about a week's worth of whiskers, came out of the house. His shirt was unbuttoned which exposed his belly that was hanging over his trousers.

He recognized Coach Williams as he stepped out of his car, and his demeanor changed immediately when he realized who he was. I was again glad that Williams was with me because I'm not sure how safe a stranger would be coming up to this house. Coach Williams introduced me to Willy Constant and told Willy that I was from LSU and wanted to talk with Logan about playing college football. Willy shook my hand, and his hand made about three of mine. I don't think I've ever seen a hand as thick and big as his.

Coach Williams told Willy that he couldn't stay, but before he left, he told him that I was a good man that he could trust and that I wanted to help so he could speak freely with me and tell me anything I needed to know. Willy then said goodbye to Coach Williams and invited me into their house.

I wasn't sure what to expect inside based on what the outside looked like, but to my amazement, the inside was very neat and clean. Willy introduced me to his wife, Loretta. She was very polite and seemed very nice. Her hair was long and stringy, and it was obvious that they didn't have much money. There were two young girls inside that were introduced as their daughters. They were told to go outside, which they did without any backtalk.

Willy told Loretta why I was there and then he said, "Mr. Scroggins, there are some things you should know about Logan."

"Really? I'm willing to listen," I said. "Logan is not really our son."

"Yes, Sir. I know. Coach Williams told me that you are his foster parents."

"Well, that's not exactly true either." Then he started telling me the real story.

2

Chapter

Willy said that Logan was Loretta's sister's son. "He's from a little place in deep Louisiana called 'Hopes Landing.' About all that's there is a fishing camp on the Atchafalaya Basin and a corrupt police department headed by Sheriff Robert Hagan. Rumor has it that Sheriff Hagan has killed many people and dumped them into the swamp for alligator bait. All the people who live there are terrified of him and his deputies. He has forced many of the women to be his sex slaves, and the men either cater to him or they disappear.

"There is only one low-lying road that goes in or out of Hopes Landing, and it floods with the high tide. So by controlling the road, the sheriff controls the village. No one has escaped from there except Logan. Somehow he waded the swamps and evaded the gators until he got past Hagan's guards. He was dripping wet and scared to death when he came knocking on our door. Mr. Scroggins, I can't begin to tell you how scared and malnourished he looked. We couldn't turn him away.

"As you can probably tell, I'm not a wealthy man. I am a logger by trade, which is not high pay to start with, and it is weather-dependent. We can't work when things are wet and muddy. But I couldn't turn him away. So you see, we are not his foster parents, but he is Loretta's nephew, and we just took him in."

I commended him on his benevolence, and then he continued talking.

"But there is more. Logan Pointer is not his real name. We agreed on that name after he got here so hopefully, no one would trace him back to Hopes Landing. As far as we know, he is the only one who can give testimony to what's happening there, and he is too scared to talk. He's been with us for almost two years, and so far, so good. Right now, all he wants to do is play football."

I told the Constants that Logan could have a bright future playing football in college with an excellent chance of making some NFL team, but I needed to talk with him because the decision to pursue this career would be his to make. They said one thing going against him was his school grades and they doubted that he could pass any of the college courses. They went on to say that he didn't have bad grades because he couldn't learn but because his emotional state was so bad when he came here that he didn't even try to study. And he soon got so far behind that he has never been able to catch up.

"I would like to talk with him if I may."

Willy said he was out back splitting firewood and that he would go fetch him. Soon, Logan came through the back door of the house and through the kitchen into the living room where I was waiting. I spoke to him and held out my hand for a handshake. He shook my hand with a firm handshake but would not look me in the eyes. He kept looking at the floor and would hardly mumble anything at all. I told him that I watched him play football a few nights ago and was impressed with how well he was able to run the ball. He shrugged his shoulders and forced out a "thanks." I asked him several easy questions, such as if he liked football and if he would like to play more after high school. Eventually, he warmed up to me somewhat and would at least look at me instead of the floor. I was able to get to the point in our conversation where I told him that I was there to see if he had any interest in playing college football for the LSU

Tigers. His first response to my question was, "Would I have to move there?"

I told him that most of the players lived there in what was called a "players dorm." I told him living in the same big house with the other players was a lot of fun and that he could make some really close friends. He said he didn't want any friends and didn't want anyone to know where he lived.

Reading between the lines, I could detect that Logan was very paranoid and feared if people knew his true identity, or where he lived, then Sheriff Hagan would come get him and take him back home - or worse still, feed him to the gators.

This boy has an enormous amount of athletic ability but it is going to be a real challenge to get him to even consider college football, much less get him to come and visit LSU. It was getting late and I needed to be leaving since I had a hot date waiting for me. I asked Logan if he would come to Baton Rouge for a visit if I could get Coach Williams to drive him over. He hesitated for a second and then said, "Probably not." I thanked them for their time and asked if it would be alright for me to come back at another time and they said I was welcome to come back at any time.

I left feeling bewildered and not knowing what I should do next. Then, I was more bewildered as I tried to find my way back to Clearwater! I thought I was paying close attention as Coach Williams led me to the Constant's house. But now, I wasn't sure which way to turn when I came to an intersection. It seemed to me that I should turn right, so I did, but after driving for what seemed to be several miles, nothing looked familiar. I kept trying to monitor my Garmin GPS but was not getting a signal. Just as I was about to turn around and go the other direction, I spotted a house and a man walking out to the mailbox. I stopped and asked him how to get back to Clearwater, and he told me to continue on in the direction I was headed and turn left at the intersection. I did as he said, and in about ten minutes, I was pulling up to the café where I was to meet my date.

I went inside to get her and introduced myself to her. She said her name was Talisa. I thought that was a beautiful name.

Talisa was a beautiful blue-eyed, black-haired Cajun girl with an olive complexion. She talked with an accent which was hard for me to understand. I asked her where she wanted to go, and she suggested going over to a friend's house where they were cooking outside and celebrating a birthday for one of their children. "A birthday party?" I asked, and she said, "Yes, a birthday party."

I was a little apprehensive as I didn't know if I was being set up to be robbed or was walking into a drug deal, or what. I really knew nothing about Talisa other than she was attractive, and I certainly didn't know anything about her friends. This was not what I had been expecting. I had figured we would go to a quiet place to eat, or maybe a movie, or someplace where it was just the two of us.

When we got to her friend's, everyone made me feel welcome and as if I was a long-lost friend. The host was a local business-man who owned an Ace Hardware Store, and they were celebrating his oldest daughter's thirteenth birthday. There was a band playing, two BBQ pit's burning, and a table full of side trimmings like coleslaw, baked beans, fried potatoes, etc. I must confess that I was pleasantly surprised and impressed.

Talisa and I got a plate of food for each of us and made our way over to a table where we listened to the music and enjoyed our meal. We had some time alone to talk, and I asked her the typical "getting to know you" questions like, "Have you always lived here? Do you have any brothers or sisters? How long have you worked at the café?" She did the same thing and asked why I was there. I told her that I was a college scout and recruiter and was looking at Logan Pointe. "Do you know him?" I asked.

She said everyone in Clearwater knew Logan because he was the football star. Then she added that she knew very little about him other than that he was a good football player. She didn't even know where he lived. I told her I had actually been to their house, but I didn't know where it was either! We both laughed at that. Then I asked, "As far as you know, has he ever been in any kind of trouble with the law or anything like that?" She said not as far as she knew, but again said she knew more "of him" than actually "about him."

Then, the conversation changed to me telling her recruiting stories from the past and eventually about my East Texas roots. It turned out to be a delightful evening. As I was leaving, I told Talisa that the next time I was back in town, I would like for us to get together again. She said she would also like that.

The next morning, I planned to head to LSU. But before I left Clearwater, I stopped by to update Coach Williams on my visit. I said, "I talked with Logan, and he has a lot of respect for you both as a coach and a person. He said he probably would not be interested in looking at LSU. Since he has so much respect for you, perhaps you can convince him to at least come and take a look." He said he would do what he could. We exchanged contact information, shook hands, and agreed to get back together soon.

As I was driving on Interstate 10 toward Baton Rouge, I couldn't shake this kid from Clearwater from my mind. I've had young men turn down my offer many times before, but somehow this one was different. While I couldn't quite put my finger on the reason, I had more of an interest in Logan than I could remember having before. Maybe I felt this was his only chance to make something of his life. Or maybe it was his past. Even though I didn't know why, there was something that kept me from giving up on him and moving on to another boy.

By early afternoon, I was meeting with the coaching staff at LSU, and we reviewed the video segments that I had sent of Logan playing against Center. I told them he had a natural instinct for the game, but he was messed up in his head. I didn't elaborate other than to say he had some emotional issues from early childhood abuse, and I wasn't sure I could get him to come here and take a look. They agreed that I should continue in my recruiting efforts.

I left unsure as to what I should do, but I felt a visit to his parents in Hopes Landing might help. I knew I would have to be extremely careful not to reveal his identity and/or location to the corrupt authorities there but I decided that I couldn't rest until I went. I left immediately.

I headed down to Donaldsonville and then took country back roads that led me deep into the swampy area of the Atchafalaya

Basin near Lake Verett. The roads were straight but narrow and heavily wooded on both sides. Because of the marshy ground, the roads were elevated, which was a good thing because much of the wooded areas were cypress trees standing in swampy water. I cringed at the thought of being out in those swamps and especially after dark. Eventually, I made my way to Hopes Landing which was, as I had been told, a small fishing village. There was a small diner on the way into town, and I stopped for a cup of coffee and hopefully some information.

I told the waitress that I was a recruiter from LSU and was looking for some big, stout, high school boys who might help our football team and it had been recommended that I look down in this part of the state. I asked her if they had a football team here, and she said they did not. I then asked her if she knew of any big strong boys. She smiled and said there may be a few of them around but that Hopes Landing only had a population of about eighteen hundred people, so the picking was going to be pretty slim. I said, "With so much swamp area around, do most of the people live right here in town?"

About that time, a local deputy came into the diner. I could tell by her change of demeanor that the waitress was scared. He made his way over to the counter where I was sitting on a barstool drinking coffee and eating a piece of coconut pie. He wanted to know what I was doing here, and I wanted to tell him that this is a free country and it wasn't any of his business why I was here but I held my tongue and told him what I had told the waitress.

Then he said, "We don't have any boys here for you, and we don't cotton too much for strangers. So the best thing for you to do is finish your pie and coffee and head back to LSU."

I told him I appreciated his advice but that I needed to at least drive through town so I could truthfully tell the LSU staff that I looked over the town and didn't see anyone who might play for us. I assured the deputy that I would not overstay my welcome.

As I finished my coffee, the deputy got a cup of his own and sat at a corner table where he continued to watch me. I felt that everything Logan had told Coach Williams about this place was exactly right. I felt very uneasy and was grateful to have the opportunity to leave. I left the diner and drove through town, which was predominately one main street with side streets that extended no more than one block. Some type of boat dock was at the end of each side street. The town was literarily surrounded by swamps. It probably took about ten minutes for me to cross town and find a gas station. I stopped and gassed up and made a brief acquaintance with the station attendant and got information on how to get to the school.

I drove by and looked at the school, but I didn't stop for fear that I was being followed and watched. I then left town with the intent of returning soon to go directly to the school with hopes of not being detected by the local sheriff's department. I got a motel room in Donaldsonville, sent an email to Coach Bevels, the head coach at LSU, and told him about my unfriendly welcome in Hopes Landing. I also told him that tomorrow, I planned to try to slip by the sheriff and visit with the high-school coaching staff if there was one. I knew they didn't have a football team, but perhaps they have a basketball or baseball team.

Then, I emailed Coach Williams and told him that I had been to Hopes Landing and was planning another trip there tomorrow. I asked if there was any way he could send me the name of Logan's parents, as I would need their signature on any scholarship agreement. Since the Constants were not Logan's legal guardians, they could not sign any letter of intent. I stressed to Coach Williams that I would keep Logan's identity and location in strictest confidence.

Later that evening, I got an email back from him with a statement that he was very apprehensive about giving me the names I needed but that he would do so. He said their last name is Beaullieu but he wasn't sure of the first names. However, he thought he remembered Logan referring to his father as "Roger." He wished me good luck. I sent Coach Williams a thank-you reply and turned on ESPN as I settled in for a night's rest.

I didn't sleep very well but was restless and tossed and turned most of the night. Finally, morning arrived, and after eating a continental breakfast, I was off again to the swamps of Hopes Landing. Before I got there, I called Dad. My step-mother, Janet, answered the phone, "Scroggins Investigative Services. This is Janet. May I help you?"

I told her who I was, and she immediately went from her professional voice to a warm family welcome. "Richard, it's so good to hear from you! Are you alright?" she asked. I assured her that everything was fine, that I was on a recruiting mission in southern Louisiana and needed to speak to Dad. She was glad to transfer me to his extension.

Soon, I heard, "Good morning. This is Robert Scroggins." "Hey, Dad!"

He was also glad to hear from me although it had only been a few days since I had seen them at Uncle Ben's funeral. After a bit of light, casual talk, I got around to my reason for calling. I told him about Logan and his rough background. I also told him about my first encounter with the Hopes Landing sheriff's department, that I was heading back there this morning to try to talk with the coach at the high school and that I wasn't sure what I was walking into.

"Dad, I don't know why this case has such a pull on me. What I should do is leave it alone and go on to the next kid, but for some reason, I can't. So if I need some private-eye type work, will you help me?"

"Son, you know I will do what I can. But you need to under-stand that you are going into a dangerous situation. Places like Hopes Landing do not welcome strangers, and it's not uncom-mon for visitors to disappear and never be seen again. During my years in law enforcement, I have heard about places like this. Richard, I think you need to back off."

"Yes, sir. I hear what you are saying, and after I talk with the coach, I may reconsider. Thanks, Dad."

"You're welcome, son. Be careful. I love you. Goodbye."

As he hung up the phone, I had an uneasy feeling that those might be the last words I would ever hear from my dad.

The road was desolate with no traffic. I wondered what a person would do if he had car trouble. I was glad I had a fairly new car which should not give me any problem. Within the hour, I was approaching Hopes Landing. I was hoping I could drive across town to the school and not be detected by the sheriff's department, and especially the fella I met yesterday. There was one four-way stop in the middle of town, and as I had suspected; when I was stopped there, a sheriff's car was approaching from the opposite direction.

3

Chapter

My heart began to race as the police car approached. Surely, there are cars that drive through town I thought. I hoped not to draw attention to myself. As I started forward from the stop sign, I passed by the deputy's car. Thankfully, it was not the same guy as before. He glared at me as we passed but he didn't stop me. Still, I felt he paid close attention to my car, and if he saw it again, it might raise a red flag. As I proceeded toward the school, I kept glancing into my rear-view mirror for any sign of the police car. Sure enough, in the distance I saw him, so I decided not to stop at the school just yet. The road I was on eventually made its way to Morgan City, so I drove out of town as if I were just passing through.

Just like the road that came into Hopes Landing, on this side of town, it was also narrow and swampy on both sides. Likewise, there was also little to no traffic. I only met one pickup truck that was heading into town. Finally, I decided to turn around but there was no good place to do so. I had to jockey around on the highway itself which took several attempts of pulling forward, backing up, and pulling forward again. Thankfully, no cars approached while I was broadside in the road.

I decided if I saw the deputy again, I would pull into the convenience store and gas up. If I didn't see him, I would head on up to the school. Vigilantly, I drove into town, and as I neared the school entrance, there was no sign of the deputy's car. I kept hoping I wouldn't be detected as I parked in front of the administration building.

I introduced myself to the receptionist and asked if I could speak with the athletic director. She said he was in class but that I could speak with the superintendent, Mr. Sanders. I agreed and was invited into his small but neat office. Mr. Sanders was cordial so long as our conversation was light, but when I started asking about potential athletes attending LSU, he was not so free with information. In fact, he said, "Mr. Scroggins, we are a small school with no athletic teams, so I don't think we would have anyone who would fit into your program. We are honored that you would consider us but we can't help you."

I thanked him for his time and wondered why they had an athletic director if they had no athletic programs. I asked that question to the receptionist as I was leaving, and she said it was a title given to the history teacher so it would increase his salary, and the school board agreed to do so.

I learned several things from this visit. For one thing, I learned the athletic director's name was Mr. Hopkins, and I knew I needed to talk with him. Secondly, I learned that the school superintendent didn't want any of his students leaving this community. Normally, a school administrator would be eager to give his students an opportunity to better themselves but that didn't seem to be the case here.

I needed to talk with Mr. Hopkins but how was I to recognize him? I decided to park where I could see the faculty parking lot and try to pick out a teacher who looked like he might be an athlete and approach him. So I sat in my car, watching the parking lot. While I waited, I texted LSU and kept them up to date on what I was doing. For one thing, I wanted them to know of my progress, but I also wanted them to know of my "whereabouts" in case I turned up missing.

I was getting hungry but didn't dare leave for fear that I'd miss Mr. Hopkins. I watched and waited and waited and watched.

Finally, school let out, but it was sometime after the busses left that the faculty left, and they trickled out one or two at a time. I saw no one who fit what I imagined Hopkins looked like. Finally, I saw a man walking out of the school that might be him, but he was being accompanied by Mr. Sanders. Since the superintendent was there, I couldn't approach the man and ask if he was Hopkins so I continued to sit and watch. They talked for a while before getting into their cars. I figured the superintendent was filling him in on my visit.

They went their separate ways, and I didn't have a chance to talk with Hopkins, so I decided to follow him. After he left the school, he pulled into the local grocery store. I drove up next to him, and while he was inside, I jotted down his license plate number and called Dad and asked him to run this number for identification. Soon, Dad called back and said the pickup was registered to Mike Hopkins, CR12, Box 33, Hopes Landing, LA. He also told me to be careful. I thanked him and then waited for Mike Hopkins to come out of the store.

After a few minutes, he returned with a few bags of groceries. As he was putting them into the back of his pickup, I approached him and said, "Excuse me, are you by chance Mike Hopkins?" He said he was, and I introduced myself to him. Right away, he seemed to be nervous as he looked in one direction and then another as if he was wondering if we were being watched.

"Could we have a minute to talk?" I asked. "Not here," he said. "Follow me home."

I agreed, and as we drove out into the countryside away from town, I wondered if I was being led into an ambush. Was Sheriff Hagan and his men out there waiting for me to become gator bait? I had to convince myself that was not the case because no one knew in advance of my contact with Hopkins. We arrived at our destination, and Mike asked me to drive my car behind his doublewide trailer so as not to be seen from the road. Then, he invited me into his home.

Once inside, he introduced me to his wife of only a few months. The two of them were very hospitable, and after giving me a sandwich and a glass of tea, we sat down at their kitchen table to talk. Mike said he was glad I was there but that I needed to watch my back. He went on to explain that this was his second year here and that he was already trapped. He said Sheriff Hagan and his deputies controlled the town and everything and everybody in it. "Once you are inside, you don't get out. That is why I asked you to hide your car. If they drove up the road and saw it in front of the house, you'd never get out."

"How can he have such a strong grip?" I asked.

"Because he is vicious and heartless and would just as soon kill you on the spot as to talk to you. People are afraid of him. He and his deputies keep tight patrol of the road in and out of town, and if anyone tries to escape, they are immediately assassinated. I had no idea it was this way until I was in too far.

"What about cell phones or internet communication?" I asked as it seemed odd to me that in this day and time, a sheriff could have such a grip.

"Mr. Scroggins, ..."

I interrupted him and said, "Call me Richard."

"Alright, Richard. Sheriff Hagan controls this town. If you are caught with a cell phone the first time, what he does is he cuts off two fingers. If you are caught a second time, you are killed. After a few were punished, no one has any cell phones." He held up his right hand and showed me where he had two fingers cut off and said, "Case in point. So no one has a cell phone. The same thing is true with computer internet. Hogan makes sure that there is no internet connection in people's houses. This place is truly unbelievable."

I was stunned by what I was hearing and asked, "What about your wife?"

Mike told me she was a local girl that he met soon after he arrived and that they fell in love and were married about a month ago. But what worries me is if Hagan decides he wants her, he will come and take her. If I try to stop him, I will be killed.

"What does the school board say about all of this?"

"The school board? That's a joke. Hagan is president of the school board and his deputies are the board members. Mr. Scroggins ..."

I interrupted him again and told him to call me Richard. "Alright, Richard. We have several boys around here who would welcome the opportunity to play football for your team but they will not be allowed to leave for fear of exposing the racket. This is really like living in prison."

"Why don't people escape by boat? When they go out fishing, why don't they just keep on going?" I asked.

"Hagan controls the fuel. Depending on where the fishermen are going, he puts only that amount of fuel in their boats. And if they venture farther than they are supposed to and fail to return at the expected time, Hagan's men go and find them and leave them at the bottom of the swamp. Richard, you really don't want to get involved in this. If you do, you will not escape."

I was amazed at what I was hearing! I couldn't imagine something like this happening in the United States at this point in time. It seemed like an episode of some horror movie.

Finally, I asked if he knew a family named Roger and Tieo Beaullieu. He said he knew of them but didn't personally know them. He added that Roger disappeared not long after he arrived as a new teacher. I asked if Tieo lived by herself, and he said she did so far as he knew except for her children. I then asked for directions to her house, and he reluctantly told me where she lives on a back road on the south side of town. I asked about the children, and Mike said there were four who range between the second and tenth grades.

After a few hours of talking, we figured it was safe for me to leave under the cover of darkness. I thanked him for his information and told him that I'd be back in touch. As I was driving in the darkness on the back road, I was very ill at ease and was just plain scared. I finally made it to the highway and was headed toward Donaldsonville when I noticed a police roadblock ahead. Now, my heart was really pounding! Had I been spotted, and were they looking for me? Or was this a routine stop that they frequently do?

Since there were no other cars on the road, I slowed almost to a stop as I approached the deputies. I rolled down my window and saw the deputy I had met the day before in the diner. He asked to see my driver's license, and after looking at it, he said, "Scroggins, I thought I told you to get out of town."

"You did and I did. Today, I am just passing through on my way back to Donaldsonville." He gave me my license back and said he didn't want to see me in this town again. He said if he did, I would be arrested for inciting a riot. I so badly wanted to ask him if it was against the law to drive through this town, but I knew I shouldn't cross him. I told him that I understood, and he let me pass.

Now, I really was confused as to what I should do. I really wanted to talk with Tieo Beaullieu but I was scared to come back. That night in the motel, I decided I would go back under disguise. I emailed my dad for advice, and he again advised me to back away and leave it alone. While I knew I should heed that advice, something kept pushing me back. The next morning, I drove back to LSU and talked with Coach Bevels. I told him that they were onto my car, so I'd like to go back in a different vehicle - perhaps, a campus pickup with no logo. He said that could probably be arranged, but he also cautioned me about the danger of getting involved in that kind of domestic lifestyle.

Then he reminded me that my job was to recruit new talent for the LSU football team, and to some degree, going to Hopes Landing was to accomplish that. But at the same time, while I was spending time and effort there, I could be but wasn't recruiting other athletes.

I understood him to be saying that I should not lose sight of my priorities and focus. I told him that I understood what he was saying, but I really thought Logan would be worth the extra effort. His reply was, "Richard, I hope you are right. Now, get out of here and be careful. Next week, I want you in someone else's living room and not in the bottom of the bayou - understand?"

"Yes, sir and thanks."

I went to the maintenance barn and signed out a Ford Ranger pickup and was soon on the road heading again toward

Hopes Landing. I put on a baseball cap and dark sunglasses in hopes of disguising my identity from a distance. As I approached the village, I could see a police car parked ahead on the side of the road. My heart began beating faster as I passed the parked car, but he stayed parked for which I was thankful. I drove across town without incident. As I was leaving town, there was another patrol car parked, and again I passed without being detected. I was so glad that I wasn't in my car. A few miles out of town, I was looking for County Road 35. Mike Hopkins said the fourth house on the right belonged to the Beaullieus and that it was about three miles down the road. Sure enough, I found CR35 about six miles out of town. Like all the other roads in this area, it was built on an elevated roadbed with swampy areas on both sides of the road. However, there were several places where the land was high enough to be out of the water, and it was in such spots that people built their houses.

I continued driving and counting houses. I drove up to the fourth house on the right, and as I drew near, I read the name *Beaullieu* on the mailbox. It was a modest frame house that was badly in need of paint. I was welcomed by several dogs, and I wasn't sure if it was safe to get out of the pick-up. But before I made my decision, a lady with long graying hair who looked to be in her mid-forties, walked out onto the front porch and commanded the dogs to be quiet. I presumed she was Tieo. They obeyed and then she spoke loudly enough for me to hear. "They won't hurt you. Who are you anyway?" "My name is Richard Scroggins, and I'm from LSU. I have some information from your sister in Clearwater. May I come in?" "Okay, Mr. Scroggins. You may get out, but you shouldn't make any sudden or threatening moves." I understood that to mean if I did, I would have to deal with her dogs. I assured her that I would be careful. I slowly made my way to the front porch where we each sat in a rocking chair.

I began by telling her that I had visited her sister and brother-in-law in Clearwater and that they were both in good health and doing well. Then I told her that I was a football recruiter and wanted to talk with her about her son coming and playing football at our school.

From reading her body language, I could tell that she was confused and didn't follow what I was saying. Then, I told her about Logan, but she didn't recognize the name because he had changed his. So I changed my tactic a little and asked if she had a son who was missing.

In tears, she said that her oldest son, Allen, disappeared a little over two years ago. "He and his papa, my husband Robert, came up missing on the same day. I've not seen or heard anything from either of them. I presume that they are dead."

I reached over and took her hand and said, "Mrs. Beaullieu, I don't know anything about your husband but your son is alive and well. He is in Clearwater with your sister. He is an outstanding football player, and I want him to come play football at LSU."

The expression on her face was one of shock and disbelief. Then she said, "My son, Allen, is alive?"

"Yes ma'am, he is. He is going by the name Logan, but he is fine." Her emotions went from disbelief to sobbing tears of joy, and she mumbled repeatedly, "My son is alive! My son is alive! Do you think my husband might also be alive?"

I told her again that I didn't know anything about her husband one way or the other.

She reached over and hugged me and said, "Thank you, Mr. Scroggins, for sharing this wonderful news with me! I can't wait to share this with others!"

I told her that she must not tell anyone for Allen's safety. I told her that he escaped the local sheriff here, and if anyone finds out he is alive, they might hunt him down and kill him. Then I asked if she understood what I was saying, and she said she did.

I went on to explain that I needed her to sign a release paper that would allow Allen to come to LSU. She said that she'd be glad to sign anything to help her son. It then hit me like a ton of bricks that I had left the necessary papers in my car when I changed into the pick-up! How stupid of me! So now, I would have to make another trip back here just to get her signature! I couldn't believe this had happened, but I didn't mention my concerns to her.

I took my phone and showed her some of the video footage I had of Logan playing football and told her that was Allen. In one segment, he was standing on the sideline with his helmet removed, and when she saw it, her eyes again filled with tears as she said, "That's my boy! That's Allen!"

While we were talking, the school bus drove up and let off her other children. They came bouncing up to the house and were curious as to who I was, and Tieo told them I was a new friend. They asked where I lived, and I told them that most of the time, I lived in Baton Rouge but that I also traveled a lot.

I got up to leave but Tieo insisted that I stay long enough to eat some sandwiches with the kids as they always thought they were starving when they got home from school. I was pretty hungry myself, so I accepted her offer. While she made the snacks, I visited with her kids and found out they all liked watching football on television. I asked them who their favorite team was, and they all said the *New Orleans Saints*. I told them that was my favorite team also, and my next favorite was the *Houston Texans*. Finally, it was time to leave, and I told Tieo that I'd be back with the papers for her to sign and she said I was welcome back anytime.

I was grateful to get back to the main road which was not as complicated as it was getting back to town from the Constant's. But when I neared the highway, there was an unexpected surprise. CR35 was blocked with county sheriff cars.

4

Chapter

When I saw the police cars, I knew by the knot in my stomach that I was in trouble. I drove up to them slowly and rolled down my window. I still had on my baseball cap and sunglasses, but that didn't help me any. The deputy looked at my driver's license and immediately asked me to step out of the pickup.

When I was outside, the deputy turned me around and cuffed me, and the deputy I had met at the diner walked up. Without any warning, he hit me in the face with his fist which almost took me to the ground. "Just couldn't stay out of our town, could you?" He then slugged me in my stomach, but this time I saw it coming and tightened my stomach muscles which helped me absorb the blow, but it still doubled me over. "Scroggins, why were you down at the Beaullieu's place?"

"I was giving her a message from her sister," I said.

He slugged me again in the face while two other deputies held me up, and he said, "That's pretty lame, Scroggins. Surely, you can do better than that. Who are you really – FBI, ATF, State Police? Who are you really working for? We need to know so we will know where to send your death notice." Then he told the other deputies to load me inside their car which they did.

I wasn't sure where they were taking me, but I knew it wasn't good. My mind was racing with thoughts on what I could say that might save my life. I kept thinking about Dad's advice to leave it alone. I wondered how they knew I was at the Beaullieu's. The only person who could have seen me there was the school bus driver. Perhaps, all of the school faculty is on the take and working as the sheriff's watchdogs.

We drove to the sheriff's office which was located in the county jail. I was taken out of the car and shoved into the office where I stood before Sheriff Hagan. He looked to be in his mid-fifties. He had a dark mustache which contrasted with the gray hair around his temples. His hair was thinning on top, and he was a little over-weight.

"Well, so you are Richard Scroggins!"

I told him I was, and he wanted to know why I was in town. Another deputy slugged me as Hagan said, "I'll ask the questions, and other than answering them, you keep your mouth shut. Is that clear?"

"Perfectly clear," I said.

"What kind of job do you have?"

I told him I was a recruiter for the LSU athletic teams. "What business do you have with the Beaullieu family?"

I told him the same thing I had told the deputies which was that I had visited her sister and was extending a message of well-being. He wanted to know where the sister lived and I told him around Lake Charles. I knew better than to say Clearwater.

He then wanted to know their names and how I met them. I didn't have good answers for either of those questions. I told him that we met casually and started talking about her childhood in a fishing village. "She said she had grown up in Hopes Landing and that she thought her sister still lived here, but she had lost touch with her. While I was driving through this area, I remembered the conversation and thought since I was here, I'd try to find the sister and tell her that her sister was doing well. I had no idea that I was in forbidden territory or that I would be beaten for merely driving through the town."

"How did you know where the Beaullieus live?" He asked.

I told him that I made my living finding out where people live. "I merely ask around until I find someone who knows who I am looking for, and they give me directions. I don't know the names of the people who work at your convenience stores." I added that in hopes they wouldn't suspect Mike Hopkins.

"Who's the head coach at LSU, and what's his telephone number?"

I told him and apparently, he wanted to know if I was telling the truth as he immediately called Coach Bevels and made up some kind of credit card survey story and said he needed to verify that I worked for his department at LSU. I could tell by his mannerism that Coach Bevels confirmed my story.

Then he said, "Mr. Scroggins, we don't like strangers snooping around our town and harassing our citizens. In fact, we don't tolerate such behavior. So, is there anything you want to say as your last testimony before you die?"

I was stunned at what I was hearing! I was about to die! I told him that many people knew where I was, and if I didn't show up at home, they would come looking for me. The sheriff calmly leaned back in his chair and said, "Scroggins, that's no problem. Your pickup will be fished out of the swamps as a one-car accident with the body missing and presumed to have been eaten by the gators. It happens all the time."

I was still in handcuffs and was very sore from the beatings when the deputies took hold of my arms and started forcing me toward the door. Just before we got there, Hagan loudly said, "Hold on just a minute!" and the deputies stopped. Then he said, "Scroggins, I believe at least part of your story is true, and I'm going to let you slide. Men, un-cuff 'im." I couldn't believe what I was hearing or what was happening as one of the deputies unlocked the handcuffs. While that was happening, Hagan said, "Scroggins, don't let me or any of my men see you in this town again - understand?"

I assured him that he made his message crystal clear. He tossed me the pickup keys and said, "Get out of my sight and out of my town!" After catching the keys, I turned and walked, or more truthfully hobbled out of the sheriff's office and got in the pickup and out of town as quickly as I could. As I drove, I counted my blessings and was thankful that I was still alive. But I knew I still needed to return to get Tieo to sign the consent and release papers for Logan to play football.

I could still just kick myself for leaving my briefcase in the trunk of the car when I took the pickup. I can't remember a time when I didn't have all the necessary papers with me when I made a house call. But then, nothing about this whole episode had been normal for me. I knew that I would have to make one more trip to Hopes Landing, regardless of the consequences, but it would not be tomorrow or any day soon.

I was trying to wrap my mind around all that had just happened. I couldn't believe that something like this could happen in America in this day and time. Perhaps, it could have happened during the Dark Ages, but today? Perhaps, the postal mail was censored, but surely someone in town had access to email or a telephone where they could notify someone of the situation. Why didn't the news media find out about the unusual happenings and have reporters swarming all over this town? How could the sheriff and deputies control people's lives? It was almost as if all the people in town were slaves. How can this be going on? Why had I never heard about it before? Almost unbelievable! And then I wondered if I should be the one to alert the FBI or whoever needed to be told. I knew the answer to that was "no" at present. I needed to keep quiet and do all I could to help get a football scholarship for a very deserving young man. Dad said he had heard about Hopes Landing, and I wondered why he had never tried to do anything to stop it.

That night, I drove all the way back to Baton Rouge and to my apartment. It was good to be home, and again I was thankful to be alive. For the first time in a long time, I paused to offer up a prayer of thanksgiving to my Heavenly Father above. It was awkward at first, but soon the words flowed easily. I promised Him that I would be more devoted to Him than I had been in the past. That night, I made the decision to refocus my life on serving the Lord as I was taught to do as a child. I knew I would have to change some of the things in my life, starting with not sleeping in on Sunday mornings. I decided I was going to attend church services every Sunday that I could. Even if I was on the road, I could seek out the church and attend.

I needed to contact Dad and Coach Bevels, but I was not in the mood to carry on a conversation with anyone tonight. I sent each of them a text message saying that I talked with Logan's mother and she was willing to sign the release papers. I told them that I had a few tense moments, but things were all right now. I told Coach Bevels that I planned to make a trip back to Clearwater tomorrow morning to watch the Panthers play again. Right now, I was emotionally drained and wanted some rest and sleep.

I tossed and turned a lot that night along with having nightmares about the judgment day before God and being tossed into outer darkness to spend eternity. I could feel myself falling helplessly into some dark vacuum. Then I'd wake up in a cold sweat. I guess my emotions were still dealing with how close I had come to dying. The next morning, I slept later than I usually did. I was sore from the beating I had received, and when I looked in the mirror, I saw that my face was badly bruised and I had what we kids used to call "a shiner" around my right eye. I couldn't see my stomach muscles, but they were extremely sore. I made a pot of coffee and sat at the small table in my kitchen area and drank it black as I ate some microwave waffles for breakfast.

About ten o'clock, I went to the campus and swapped the pickup for my car, and I was very glad to see my briefcase with all the papers in it. I was soon on Interstate 10 heading for Clearwater. I figured I would be there about mid-afternoon which would give me time to check into a motel and have a few hours before the Clearwater Panthers hit the gridiron. After I checked in, I went to the little café to see if Talisa was there, and to my good fortune, she was.

When she saw me, she immediately asked what had happened to my face. I told her it was just part of the dangers of my job and that I would explain later. I asked if she was free tonight, and she said she was and that she got off work at five. I invited her to go with me to the football game. I told her that she could tag along and see what I do for a living, and I promised her that she wouldn't get hurt. She said she rarely went to a football game and didn't know much about it, but that she would like to go with me. She agreed to come by the motel, and we could leave from there.

She arrived at the motel before it was time to leave for the game which gave us a little time to visit. I told her that I had been in a small town trying to recruit a football player. The police department didn't appreciate my being there so they convinced me that I wasn't welcome and invited me to leave which I did. She was shocked and said that was police brutality and should be reported to the authorities. I assured her that it was best not to make a big deal of it at this time. I told her that I left town and that should be the end of it. She was still pretty bothered by the whole thing.

We had a little time for me to explain some of the rules of a football game to her. I told her I would give her a "press pass" and she could sit with me in the press box. I also told her that I needed her help in keeping some stats on one of the players, and she laughed as she asked me what a *stat was*. I gave her a logbook and explained that I wanted her to write for me each time Logan carried the ball and how many yards that carry included. She said she could do that. We soon arrived at the football stadium and went up to the press box as we were both wearing "press badges." As we were getting settled, two high-school girls came into the press box from the concession stand and asked if we wanted to order anything. Talisa was impressed with that and laughingly said that I was being pampered. We looked at the program and I showed her Logan's number and told her that he was the one she needed to watch.

Before long, the game started, and we got down to business. I was watching and videoing Logan while Talisa was logging his yardage. She seemed to be enjoying herself, and occasionally she would stand up and yell, "Go, go, go!" This got the attention of the others in the press box, especially the radio announcers, because normally the people in the press box are all business and keep their emotions to themselves during the game. As much as she was enjoying the game, I suspected that she might become a loyal fan. Logan had another outstanding performance, and I was convinced more than ever that he could be the star that could turn the LSU football program around. After the game, I made my way to the locker room and was quickly spotted by Coach Williams. He motioned for me to go to his office but I declined and mouthed to him, "Tomorrow – can we talk?" He nodded.

I found Logan and told him that I enjoyed watching him run and would like to come and visit with him tomorrow afternoon. He seemed to be undecided about that, but I assured him that I would not try to persuade him to do anything that he didn't want to do.

Then, I noticed him staring at my face. I said, "Courtesy of the Hopes Landing Sheriff's Department." He seemed surprised that I had been there and seemed to be scared as well. I told him not to be afraid because everything was alright, but that we needed to talk. I then asked again if we could get together tomorrow afternoon, and this time he agreed.

On the way back to the motel, Talisa said she couldn't remember when she had so much fun and really appreciated me inviting her to go with me. I told her it was my pleasure and I had also enjoyed the evening much more because she was with me. I suggested that we become a team and go to another game next Friday night. She said that she'd love to but didn't know her work schedule.

There was a McDonald's Restaurant across the street from my motel, and we went there for something to drink and for more conversation. I found out that she grew up in Pasadena which was just outside of Houston. I told her that my dad used to be a policeman in southeast Houston and his precinct bordered Pasadena. I remembered living in Houston when I was a small boy, but then Dad moved us back to east Texas, which is where he grew up. I was grateful that he did because I thought growing up in the country was much better than growing up in a city. Talisa agreed. I asked her if she had a steady fella, and she said she was dating someone, but that he worked offshore and was only home a few days out of the month. I asked her if she had ever been married and was pleased to hear that she hadn't. She said she had been engaged once when she lived in Pasadena, but it didn't feel right and that she backed out two weeks before the wedding date. Then, she reversed the questions on me, and I told her that I had never had a serious relationship. I noticed she smiled when I said that.

Eventually, the conversation worked its way to me being in Hopes Landing. I told her that I was following up on a football prospect named Allen Beaullieu and that the local sheriff saw me as a threat. I watched her carefully when I said his name to see if it touched any kind of nerve, and it seemed that it didn't. I definitely didn't want her to suspect Allen and Logan were the same person. "I went there asking questions and that raised a flag so they caught me last night, roughed me up, and then ordered me out of their town."

"Well, did you recruit the player? "she asked.

"I'm not sure yet. I'm still working on it." I wanted to tell her the whole story but I didn't dare for fear that the word about Logan's true identity might come out, and if it did, it was not going to be because of me.

Finally, it was late. We walked across the street to the motel, and then she got into her car to go home. I kissed her good night through the window, and again she told me that she had a great time and then drove off. For some reason, I hated to see her go.

Since I hadn't slept much the night before, I hit the sack pretty quickly and before long, I was out like a light.

The next morning, I was awakened by the normal motel sounds of people coming and going, doors slamming, and cars starting. I felt I was moving in slow motion like an old man, but after a quick shower, I began to function. By nine o'clock, I was walking into Coach Williams' office. "Come in, Scroggins. I was looking at the video of last night's game. It's always easier to watch these things when you win." He turned off the machine and asked me to have a seat across the desk from him. "Find out anything?" He asked.

I told him about my visit to Hopes Landing and pointed to my face as testimony that I was there. "I was able to find Logan's mother. His daddy is presumed dead, and she is more than willing to sign a release for him to play college ball. She thought he was also dead, and the fact that he is alive brought new life to her. All we need to do now is convince Logan to go take a look at our campus." Coach Williams said a recruiter from the University of Houston was here last week, but he thought he discouraged him enough that he wouldn't give me any competition. "What did ya tell him?" I quizzed.

"I told him that Logan was planning to go to LSU and there was no use for him to pursue it any further." I was pleased to hear that. I believed the coach was on my side.

"Coach, next weekend I have to make a trip to east Texas for a family wedding, but the weekend after that, do you think you could get Logan to LSU?"

He answered by saying, "I don't know if I can or not, but I will try. As far as my schedule is concerned, that's not a problem. In fact, that would be a perfect time for me as we have an off week that weekend. If I can persuade him to go, we could be there on Friday night."

We then started talking about last night's game, how well the guys played as a team and especially how well Logan ran the football. Coach commented that Logan seemed to have a natural instinct on when to make a cut or kick the speed into high gear. I agreed with him and added that the thing I liked was that no one player could tackle him. It takes at least two, and most of the time three or more, to get him down. "That's what we need at LSU."

After about an hour or so, I told Coach Williams that I planned to go visit Logan again. He asked if I remembered the way, and I had to confess that I wasn't too sure, but I thought so. He drew me a map just in case.

I stopped by the café for a quick lunch before heading out to the Constant's place, and Talisa was on duty. When she saw me come in, she made sure that she waited on me. One of the first things she said was that she had to work next weekend. I told her that was fine because I received a text message this morning reminding me of my cousin's wedding in East Texas, and I'm supposed to be one of his groomsmen. "I'm glad they reminded me because I had forgotten all about it."

But I did make a date with her for tonight and got a "maybe" on my invitation for her to attend church services with me in the morning. Then I was off to the boonies.

With the help of my hand-drawn map, I found the Constant's house without any trouble. It seemed that Logan had told them I was coming because they were waiting for me. Loretta had some iced tea on the table along with a plate of warm chocolate chip cookies. Even though I had just eaten, I did not refuse her hospitality.

Logan was sitting in the living room with us as I told them that I had found his mother. I told them that she had thought Logan was dead, and when she found out he was alive, she was beside herself with joy. I explained that she told me Logan's real name was *Allen,* and she was excited about the possibility of him playing football at LSU. I assured them that I did nothing or said anything that would jeopardize his identity or location.

"Logan, your mother said this would be a chance for you to make something of your life and to do something that would bring your family honor and respect. She agreed to sign the release papers for you to play football at LSU. Son, won't you at least come to the campus and take a look? Coach Williams has agreed to drive you up there, and your aunt and uncle are welcome to come with you. Will you come?"

"Mr. Scroggins, I'm sorry you got beat up and I'm glad my mother knows that I'm alive and alright. But I'm afraid I won't be able to meet your expectations of me. I don't think I'm good enough."

"Logan, I'm not asking the impossible of you. I'm not even asking you to be exceptional. All I'm asking is for you to come and try out.

And if you make the team, then play like you play at Clearwater - no more than that. Will you at least give it a try and not disappoint your mother?

"Maybe. Let me think about it. But I want you to know that I'm scared. I'm scared that I can't perform but I am more scared that Sheriff Hagan will recognize me and come after me because I know what they did to my daddy."

"Did you see them kill your daddy?" I asked.

"No, but I overheard them arguing over the killing of alligators, and my dad told them he wasn't going to have anything to do with it because it was wrong and against the law to poach gators. I guess they sell the skins to people to make shoes and boots and stuff. I remember Sheriff Hagan laughing and saying, 'Roger, I am the law around here, and you best remember it.' That's when my dad said, 'We'll see about that' and turned to get back into his boat. Two deputies grabbed him and handcuffed and pushed him into their boat. As they were headed out into the swamp, one of them spotted me hiding behind some oil barrels. They yelled back to the sheriff, "The kid! He's behind the barrels!" The sheriff said, "That's okay. We'll get him later. I know where he lives." That's when I broke and ran and jumped into the water and swam as hard as I could to try to get through the swamps and out of Hopes Landing. I wanted to follow the boat and see what they did with my dad, but they were long gone. I just know they tossed him into the swamp - and all because he refused to help them do something that is illegal. I remembered Aunt Loretta lived at Clearwater, and I walked and ran and hid and walked and ran and hid some more. I finally got to her house, but I hadn't eaten anything for days and was so very tired. I knew my mom would be worried but I also knew I would have been killed if I had stayed there. I couldn't send her a letter telling her where I am because the mail carriers work for the sheriff and they open and read letters that are sent to people living there. Not many people are allowed to have a telephone."

Logan broke down in tears as he stopped his testimony. I could understand how he would be afraid that Hagan would get him if he knew where he was. I gave him a pat on the back and told him I was proud of him and that I would make sure that his true identity was kept quiet. I also told him to think seriously about what I had said as I thought he could have a bright future playing the game he loved to play.

That night, Talisa and I had a quiet dinner at her trailer. She lived in an old, but very neat and clean, mobile home. It was in a well-kept trailer park that was pretty impressive with a playground, swimming pool, and recreation building for its residents and their guests. The evening was perfect. After we ate lasagne, we settled down and watched a rerun of "Forrest Gump".

I was pleased that Talisa's "maybe" turned into a "yes" and that she went to church with me the next morning. We both enjoyed the service, and she said she hadn't gone to church since she was a little girl. I admitted that I had not been as faithful as I should have been or that I planned to be again.

She had the day off from work, and we got a wild hair and decided to go to East Texas for a surprise visit to my folks and to show her some of the places that I had been talking about. The drive seemed to pass quickly as our conversation flowed easily. We laughed and joked a lot over silly things, and I realized that I really enjoyed her company. I felt a little tug at my heartstrings when I remembered that she had a "somewhat" boyfriend.

Dad and Janet were almost in a state of shock when they answered the knock on their door and saw us standing there. They welcomed us with open arms, and I was glad to introduce them to Talisa. Janet said, "If I knew you were coming, I'd a baked a cake" and sang it to the tune of that old song. We laughed and she said she could give us some peanut butter and jelly sandwiches instead. Talisa joined in the jovial mood and said she would prefer a sandwich any day to a piece of cake.

I could tell Dad was eager to talk to me about the conversation we previously had about Hopes Landing but he was also wise enough not to mention it in front of Talisa as he didn't know what she knew and what she didn't. He did ask about the bruises on my face, and I told him I was in the wrong place at the wrong time. Janet wanted to know if I had gone to a doctor. I told her that I was tough and didn't need a doctor.

The afternoon passed quickly, and Talisa seemed to be very much at ease around my family. That made me happy. Of course, we talked about the upcoming wedding and that I would be back next weekend to be a part of those festivities. They invited Talisa to come back with me, and she thanked them for the invitation but said that would be her weekend to work. They told her she would be welcome to come at any time. She smiled her beautiful smile that showed pearly-white teeth.

Since we had a long drive back home, we hugged each other and said our goodbyes and headed back to Louisiana. As we were driving back to Clearwater, we talked a lot about family and family values. We were tooling along down the road when, all of a sudden, a deer ran across the road in front of an oncoming car. The car swerved to avoid the deer and crossed over into our lane. All I saw were headlights coming toward me at 65 mph!

5

Chapter

I could hear the dogs closing in on me as I sloshed through the murky water. I was too exhausted to run anymore, so I crawled up on the base of a cypress tree and watched the flashlights slowly making their way through the darkness of the night coming toward me. I didn't care anymore if they caught me or not! Soon, they were close enough that I could hear their voices. Then one said, "There he is!" Immediately, I was blinded by flashlights shining in my face. I was scared. I knew my life would soon be over as I heard the rattle of chains and Sheriff Hagan saying, "I told you to keep away from these parts! Now we will make sure that you do!" Then one of his deputies grabbed my arm, and I instinctively fought back.

"Mr. Scroggins, calm down before you pull your I.V. out!" I looked and saw a nurse standing beside me. I was confused and asked where I was. She told me that I was in the Angelina County Medical Center recovering from an auto accident.

"Auto accident?" I mumbled. "When?"

By this time, the room was full of medical people checking me out. They were looking at my head, into my eyes, asking questions such as 'what is your name?' After what seemed to be hours of interrogations, a man I presumed to be a doctor stood beside me and said, "Mr. Scroggins, I am Dr. Stinson. Do you know where you are and why you are here?" I told him I had no idea except that the nurse said I had been in an auto accident.

He explained to me that about three weeks ago I was involved in a head-on crash on Highway 69 just a few miles out of town. He said I had a broken shoulder, several cracked ribs, and a head injury. As he talked, I realized that I had been having a dream about being in the swamps and being chased by Sheriff Hagan - but it seemed so real.

Dr. Stinson continued, "The head injury has been our biggest concern. Naturally, with an impact to the head like that, follows a lot of swelling and bruising and often a loss of memory along with the loss of motor skills. The fact that you can talk with me is a very good sign. It's also a good sign when you were fighting with the nurse because it shows that you can still use your arms. Your ribs and shoulder are healing nicely but will continue to be sore for a while longer. There is someone here who wants to see you. I'll be back later to check on you."

As he stepped aside, I saw Janet, my stepmom, standing across the room. She had a tissue in her hands that she was using to wipe tears from her eyes. Soon, the room was empty of all the people except Janet. As she came toward me, I tried to turn to look at her and realized that the pain in my ribs was excruciating.

"Hey!" I said.

With trembling lips, she mumbled, "Hey yourself! How are you feeling?"

"I don't know, but I know that it hurts to move."

"We have been so concerned about you and were afraid you wouldn't come out of your coma. It is so wonderful that you are awake and able to talk. God has really answered our prayers."

Then, I asked her what happened. She explained that I was driving on the highway, and from what they could figure out, a car swerved into my lane and hit me head-on. There were no skid marks, so apparently, there was no attempt by that driver to stop by hitting his brakes.

As she talked, I started to remember. I remembered a deer crossing the road between me and the other car. Then, without warning, the car came right at me. The last thing I remember seeing was bright lights on my face. "What about the people in the other car?" I asked.

Janet said they had both died. The driver was killed on impact, and his wife died later that night in the hospital. Then she asked, "Richard, do you remember where you had been and why you were on that road?"

I thought and thought but could not get a grip on why I was driving there that night.

"Richard, do you remember Talisa?" I had no idea who Talisa was. Then, she asked me if I remembered what I did for a living and what project I was working on but I didn't know.

"Richard, we are so glad and thankful that you are alive and awake! I'm going to make a few phone calls and share this good news with your daddy and others. I'll be back later." She leaned over and kissed me on the cheek and told me that she loved me. I was so glad she was my stepmom.

After Janet left, I lay there trying to remember some of the things she mentioned but all I could get in my mind was the dream of me being in the swamp and about to die. My thoughts were interrupted by a nurse who came to take my order for lunch. I hadn't thought about eating, but now that we were talking about it, I realized that I was hungry. I ordered mashed potatoes and cream gravy with toast, but the best part was some Bluebell ice cream. While I waited for my food, I kept trying to remember Talisa and what relationship, if any, we had.

I dozed off to sleep again and had another nightmare. It was similar to the one before. I was being chased in the swamps by a group of lawmen who were trying to kill me. They had chains around my neck, and my hands were tied as I was being taken out into deep water. I was struggling to no avail. Then they tossed me over into the murky water, and I was quickly sinking toward the bottom. I then woke up in a cold sweat, and I could tell that my pulse rate was high. The nurse came in, and as soon as she saw me, she called for assistance.

Soon the RN on duty came in and began to check my vital signs while asking me questions. They soon figured out that I was having anxiety attacks stemming from my dreams. After a few more questions about my dreams, they made arrangements for me to receive psychological therapy.

"Am I going crazy?" I asked. They assured me that I wasn't, but after a head trauma, sometimes hallucinations and traumatic dreams will occur. They assured me that I had nothing to worry about and that things would get better in time.

While I was eating, Janet returned and told me that my dad was on his way and would be here soon. She and I talked, and I told her that I didn't remember a lot of stuff but I kept having terrible dreams about being drowned in a swamp. She said she could help me with some of the things I didn't remember but she couldn't do anything about the dreams.

She told me that I was a sports recruiter for the LSU Tigers and that I lived in Baton Rouge, La. I was trying to recruit a high school football player from the Lake Charles area. While there, I met a girl named Talisa, and the two of us were on our way back to Lake Charles after visiting her and Dad in East Texas.

As she talked, some of it sounded vaguely familiar but I couldn't quite get it all together. While we were talking, Dad came in. It was so good to see him, and with tears running down his cheeks, he came over to my bed and hugged me and said in a cracking voice, "Son, I'm so thankful … (pause to clear his throat) … thankful that you are alive and awake. I … (another brief pause) … I was afraid I might never have the opportunity again to tell you that I love you." I didn't know what to say. I just hugged him back and said, "I know. Me too." After he moved away and regained his composure, he pulled a chair up near my bed, and we began to talk. He asked how much I remembered about my recruiting project, and I told him that I didn't remember anything about it nor that I was a recruiter until Janet told me. He asked me if *Hopes Landing* rang a bell. It sorta did, but I couldn't get that together either. Then, he told me that Hopes Landing was a corrupt town with a corrupt sheriff's department and that I had gone there to work on a recruiting project. He said they had beaten me up, run me out of town and told me to never come back there again.

I vaguely remembered getting beat up, and I could see the sheriff in my mind as being the same sheriff in my dreams. I told Dad about my dreams and that the sheriff that beat me up was the same fella I was dreaming about. He went on to tell me that he also went to Hopes Landing while I had been here in the hospital. He said he drove through as a tourist fisherman and stopped at a convenience store for gas and something to eat. "While I was there, a sheriff's deputy drove by twice. As I looked out the window, he came by a second time and wrote down my license plate number. I figured that might happen, so I put an extra set of plates on my car that I had registered to a bogus name through the detective agency. I didn't want anyone to run my plate and see it registered to someone named Scroggins. That would have certainly raised a flag. As I was driving out of town, a deputy followed me all the way to the city limits sign where he pulled over on the side of the road and parked."

I could see a mental picture of the town, but still had a hard time remembering why I was there and any details of what happened there. After a while of visiting with Dad and Janet, he said they were going out for a bite to eat but would be back later.

After they left, I dozed off to sleep and had a good nap without a bad dream. The next thing I remembered was waking up to a nurse checking my vitals and taking my supper order.

Later that evening, Dad and Janet came back in with Talisa. I recognized her immediately and had full recall of our conversations! Then I also remembered the wreck and the blinding lights. I asked her if she was hurt in the accident. She said she only sustained a few bruises because I swerved to the right, and the oncoming car hit us broadside on the driver's door. She told me she had been very worried about me and was praying that I would come out of the coma and be able to remember things.

I told her that some things were coming back while others were still sketchy. I told her when Janet mentioned the name *Talisa*, I couldn't put the name with a face but when I saw her walk through the door, I knew immediately who she was and what her name was. "How have things been going with you and the café?" I asked.

"Things have been going quite well other than my worrying about you. I talked with your folks every day to see if there had been any changes in your condition and was happy today when I was told that you were awake." She reached over and grabbed my hand and said, "Richard, I can't tell you how joyful that made me feel. I immediately knew I had to make arrangements for someone to cover for me at work because I wanted to come and see you."

I told her I was glad she came and that I hoped she would come often. Then she told me two other things that thrilled me. One was that she had broken things off with her boyfriend, and secondly that she had continued to go to church where we went together. She told me that I was remembered in prayer at every service.

While we were talking, there was a tap on the door. Dad went to the door and in walked Coach Williams and Logan! When I saw Logan, everything immediately snapped back into place in my mind. I remembered visiting his home and how he had escaped Hopes Landing. I remembered visiting with his mother. I remembered it all. It is truly amazing how the human mind works.

Coach Williams said he had some good news for me, and naturally, I was curious as to what that might be. He asked if I remembered the date we had set to visit LSU. I told him I did but I guess I missed it. He said I did indeed miss it, but that he and Logan had gone on without me.

"And?" I felt I had to drag the rest out of him.

"And we met with the athletic staff there, talked with some of the players, took a tour through the campus and athletic dorm, and Logan loved it! The players made him feel welcome and special. They talked about how they could hardly wait for him to come and be a part of their team. Scroggins, to make a long story short, Logan signed a letter of intent to attend LSU. The only thing lacking is the consent paper from his mother."

"Wow! That is great news! Logan, what changed you thinking?" I asked.

"It was your wreck. I kept thinking about how you cared enough about me to go to Hopes Landing and got beat up, how you visited with my mama, and how you were trying to help me have a better life. No one had ever shown that kind of interest in me, and when I heard that you were hurt real bad in a car wreck and might not live, I knew what I needed to do. Mr. Scroggins, it was you who changed my thinking, and I want to thank you."

Naturally, I was choked up and told him that I was very proud of the decision he had made and that I felt sure he would not regret it. I smiled to myself at his misuse of some words, but he had said what he wanted to say.

They didn't stay very long as they all felt I needed some rest. I was so appreciative of every visitor and especially the news about Logan's decision. One by one they left the room - Coach Williams and then Logan followed by Janet and Dad.

Talisa was the last to leave. Before leaving, she came to my bedside, kissed me on the cheek and said, "Richard, this may seem strange to you, but like Logan, when I realized that there was a possibility of you dying and that I might not be able to see you again, I was so afraid. Although I have only known you for a short time, I realized that I love you, and I don't think I could go on without you in my life. There! Now I said it, and you probably think I'm crazy, but that's the way I feel."

"No, I don't think you are crazy. Talisa, I am very fond of you as well, and I would certainly have a good life with you in it." She then said goodnight and that she would be back soon. After she left, I pondered about what she had said. I was very comfortable with her, but I wasn't sure my feelings for her were as strong as hers were for me. However, I was very happy when I was with her, and she seemed to fit in well with my family. I realized I didn't want to move into a permanent relationship too quickly only to wake up one day and realize that I had made a mistake.

I slept better that night as I was given an anti-anxiety pill which helped tremendously with my nightmares. The next morning, which I was told was Saturday, Dad came back to see me. He was by himself which was a bit unusual. He brought me a cup of hot, black coffee and also had one for himself. We sat and drank our coffee as we talked and before long, our conversation centered on *Hopes Landing*.

"Son, after I went there, I came away feeling that place was purgatory on earth. I could feel corruption in the air and could sense the fear in the people. We need to decide what we need to do."

"We? Did you say what *'we'* need to do?"

"That's right. I feel the need to get involved, and between the two of us, perhaps, we can put a stop to what is going on there."

I asked him what decision we needed to make. He said we should decide to either back away and leave it alone, which was the safest and easiest thing to do, or to just figure out a strategy to shut 'em down. I told him that I wanted to shut 'em down, but for the next few weeks, I was going to be out of commission. Dad said that would probably play in our favor as their antagonism toward me might settle down when they didn't see me hanging around their town.

Dad left with plans to drive back through Hopes Landing in order to get a better scope of the place. After that, he thought we could put together a plan that might work. After he left, I was worried about him getting involved. But then again, he was a private investigator and had been in dangerous situations many times before. He knew how to take care of himself as he had done many times in his line of work.

The weeks were passing slowly even though I had many visitors. My sister, Rachael, who lives outside of Austin, came to see me. Coach Bevels dropped by one afternoon and was bragging about what a good prospect for the football team that Logan seemed to be. Talisa came by several times a week and I found myself becoming more and more fond of her. In fact, I felt an attachment to her like I had never felt before. But I still didn't know if it was "love" that I was feeling.

Finally, I had finished all the psychological treatments and my body had healed to the point that I was released from the hospital. I was thankful that the couple who hit me had good auto insurance that paid for all of my medical expenses. I marvelled that insurance companies can stay in business after I saw the itemized list of what my medical expenses were – a little over one and a half million dollars!

Rather than going back to my apartment and taking care of myself alone, I decided to go stay with Janet and Dad for a few days. While I was there, they waited on me almost hand and foot. During the day, they were at their office, but all the other times they pampered and spoiled me. I rather liked that!

One afternoon, Darrin; my stepbrother, stopped by while Dad and Janet were at the office, and we had a good visit. It had been a long time since I had spent any quality time with him. He was in law school at the University of Texas and was living not too far from Rachael. We discussed my situation, and he confirmed what I already knew. He said without solid evidence, it would be hard to shut Sheriff Hagan down because the legal system almost always leans in favor of the law enforcement agencies.

Later that day, Darrin and I went to the office where he spent a few minutes with Janet and Dad before heading back to Austin. After he left, Dad invited me into his office where he began to lay out his plan to Janet and me.

6

Chapter

Janet and I sat in the office chairs across from Dad's desk. He walked from behind his desk and sat on the front corner near us.

He said, "I want to tell you what I have been thinking".

Then, he explained that after he drove back through Hopes Landing and stopped at the local café, he thought he had a pretty good feel of the lay of the land. To my surprise, he pulled out pictures he had taken while he was there and said no one had a clue he had taken them. He showed me his ring which looked like a large college ring, but instead it was really a small camera. Underneath the finger, he pushed the ring band with his thumb and it silently snapped a picture. As we were talking, he told me he had just snapped my picture twice, and I suspected nothing.

"Hey, Dad! You're pretty good! You should be a private detective when you grow up!" We all laughed.

He said that in his line of work, you have to be good to be successful and you have to keep up with the latest electronic gadgets and technology to be effective. He had pictures of the café waitress that I had talked with along with Sheriff Hagan and three deputies. After I saw the pictures, I was ready to listen to his plan. He said he wanted to get the FBI involved and had several friends with the agency who would be willing to help us. He said we couldn't just storm the place and make a massive raid and arrests because of the lack of concrete evidence. Hagan has done a pretty good job of covering his tracks.

"I think what we need to do is infiltrate them with some high-tech recording devices and force them to divulge what they are doing. Because of his arrogance, I think if you push the right buttons, Sheriff Hagan will boast about his activities. We will have a team nearby monitoring the conversation, and as soon as we get recorded testimony that will stand up in court, we can move in quickly and make the arrest."

I wanted to know where the team would be while they waited to make their move. Dad said he saw a couple of abandoned-looking driveways just a few miles out of the city limits which looked like they would hold two or three cars. In addition, a utility van, possibly two, with some bogus plumbing logo painted on the side could be parked in the grocery store parking lot. Each van can hold up to ten agents in addition to the surveillance recording equipment.

My next question was "who was going to be the guinea pig", although I already knew the obvious answer. Dad just smiled when I asked him.

Then, he explained more specifically. He wanted me and an FBI agent to go back into town, and after we were arrested and brought before Hagan, we should try to get him to talk. We will have recording devices on us that will capture everything he says.

"What if they search us and find the wire?" I asked.

"They won't find "the wire" because we don't use wires anymore," Dad said as he held up his hand and pointed to his ring. "You will have a recording ring, and the agent will have a camera ring. Believe me - they will not know what you are doing."

My next question was "when." Dad said we were several weeks away as it would take some time to get things coordinated with his FBI friends who would really take the lead in this operation. It would take time to get the vans equipped and painted, etc., which meant it may be two months out. I figured that was a good thing as it would give me more time to heal from my injuries. I was also amazed at what he was telling me. It was so good that he had agreed to help with this endeavor, or else my nightmares would probably come true and I would end up in the bottom of the swamp.

I didn't have any more questions, nor did Janet, so they ordered pizza for supper and we headed home.

That night, I kept playing out our plan in my mind. I tried to imagine this and that and what I'd do in case different things happened. It was comforting to know that this time, I'd have someone with me. And then, my thoughts shifted to Talisa. Should I tell her about all of this? As much as I wanted to, I really felt it best not to involve her. As a matter of fact, I really didn't know much about her other than what she told me, and I trust that she was telling me the truth. In an absurd way, she might have some link to Sheriff Hagan and that's why she was coming on to me so strong. I convinced myself that I was letting my mind get out of control and that there was no way she could be involved with Hagan. But still, I wondered.

After a few more days at home, it was time for me to go back to Baton Rouge. Dad promised to keep me in the loop as things progressed. Naturally, I went to Baton Rouge by way of Lake Charles. Talisa was working but came and joined me for a few minutes during her break. It was so good to see her, and I wondered how I could have ever thought about her being involved in all of the Hopes Landing stuff. But I still believed I should not tell her about anything that was planned.

After leaving the café, I drove out to see Logan and the Constants. They were glad to see me and the progress I had made with my health. Logan reaffirmed to me his commitment to attend LSU which I was glad to hear, and I re-emphasized to him that he was making a good decision. I just knew within me that he would have a bright future as a football star.

Eventually, I made it back to my apartment where I had almost two months of mail to sort through plus tons of email messages. After what seemed to be several hours, I finally worked through it all and ended up throwing away and discarding most of it. I called Coach Bevel, and he dropped by to catch me up on all that was happening in the recruiting department. He said we had sixteen boys who had committed to coming to LSU, but no one stood out quite like Logan. I agreed that he was one-of-a-kind that doesn't come along very often. Then, Coach Bevel reminded me that we still needed the consent papers from Logan's mother. I told him that I would work on getting them as soon as I could, but it might be after Christmas, which was only a few weeks away because I could not be released from the doctor to return to work until January.

Later that night, I thought about writing to Logan's mother, but I feared the letter might get intercepted and Sheriff Hagan would learn that Logan was alive so I dismissed the idea. I considered slipping into their town at night, but as sure as I did, I would get caught and that would be the end of me and the plan Dad has in mind. I finally reconciled myself to waiting until everything was in place before going back to Hopes Landing.

While I lay in bed thinking about things that needed to be done, I received a telephone call from Talisa. I could tell by her voice that she was frantic. I asked her what was wrong, and she said the café was on fire. "Trucks and firemen are everywhere, but the building is completely destroyed! I don't know what I'll do without a job. I won't be able to pay rent, buy groceries, or put gas in my car. Oh, Richard! What can I do?"

I told her to remain calm and not make any decisions in a panic. I suggested that she go to her home and that I'd drive over tomorrow and help her sort all of this out. We talked for several more minutes, and she seemed a little more rational when we hung up. Now my focus was on Talisa and not Hopes Landing.

Lake Charles was about three hours away, and I left early since I was still on medical leave from work. By mid-morning, I was at Talisa's. As we sat around her kitchen table, she said she didn't get any sleep for trying to figure out what to do. The café was a total loss, and the owner at this point wasn't sure what he would do either. Even if he rebuilds, she said she was looking at several months, if not a year, without a paycheck.

The obvious solution was to get another job, but she seemed reluctant to do that. What she really wanted to do was move in with me, but I discouraged that because it is not morally right. Regardless of how society views it, living together outside of marriage goes against God's principles, and she agreed with me. But I would not be opposed to her moving to Baton Rouge to find work and live closer to me. I couldn't understand why looking for another job seemed to bother her so much.

Finally, it came out. She told me that she had not told me everything about her past. She said she had a felony charge against her and had spent eighteen months in the Texas prison system. Because of her record, it was hard to get a job and she preferred that people not know about her past.

I was shocked at what I was hearing and naturally wanted to know what happened. Then she began to explain.

"While living in Houston, I was nineteen and reckless. I picked some bad friends, and one night, we were all drinking and decided it would be exciting to rob a convenience store. There were two boys and two other girls that I knew from high school. As far as I know, none of us had ever done anything like that before. We did it, and before we left the parking lot, the place was surrounded by police. The store clerk must have sounded an alarm somehow. Well, the rest is history. I got the lightest sentence because I just stood in the doorway and really was not an active participant so I was guilty more by association than participation. But I served some time which I will never be able to erase from my past. Every job application requires a criminal background check and I don't want to lie about it so I prefer not to apply."

I was amazed at what I was hearing and said, "Talisa, I realize what happened was a long time ago, and I understand. I want you to know that this doesn't change how I feel toward you. We all have things in our past that we'd like to forget or undo if we could, but sometimes there are consequences to the choices we make, and we can't change them. This is one of those things, but we should try to move forward. How did you get the job at the café?" I asked.

"Mr. Soliska, the owner, had a 'help wanted' sign on the door. I walked in and talked with him about it, and he hired me on the spot without me ever filling out an application. I have worked for him for six, almost seven, years."

Well, all of this certainly took me by surprise. I wondered if there were other things about her that I needed to know if we were to have a long-term relationship. After talking for several hours, I agreed to pay her next month's rent and leave her some grocery money in order to give us a little bit of time to figure out what to do. We drove by the café and it was roped off to unauthorized people, but Talisa saw Mr. Soliska standing across the way talking with who we assumed to be either an investigator or an insurance adjuster. She got his attention, and after a few minutes, he made his way over to us. Talisa hugged him and they both had tear-filled eyes. Mr. Soliska was a man who appeared to be in his late sixties. He was short and chubby. He talked with a strong Polish accent and said, as he pointed to the ashes behind him, "Dis was my life. Now tis gone. What I'll do, I don't know."

Talisa asked if they knew how the fire started. She feared but hoped it was not arson. In his broken English, Mr. Soliska said, "Christmas lights. They think it was from bad Christmas lights." He went on to explain that he was underinsured and wasn't sure he could afford to rebuild.

We left there and went to the grocery store. I told Talisa that I'd catch up with her as I had a few phone calls that I needed to make. While she was inside, I called Dad and told him what had happened and about what Talisa had told me. He said he would do a background search to see if there was anything else about her that we should know. I appreciated that and then asked him if she could possibly move up there and maybe work for them until she could get a little bit of direction as to what to do and where to go. Dad immediately said that he could put her to work as office help, but she would not be paid much above minimum wage. Then he quickly added, "She should be able to get by on that because she could stay with us with room and board as additional compensation." I felt that was more than generous and thanked him again and again. I realized one more time what a wonderful and caring family I had. I wondered if Talisa even had any family. I couldn't remember her mentioning anyone.

I rushed inside the store and found Talisa with only four or five things in her shopping cart. I pulled her aside to a table in the small deli that was in the corner of the store. I could hardly wait to tell her the news I had! She was ecstatic and couldn't believe what she was hearing! I told her to return the grocery items, and I'd help her pack her things and we'd drive to East Texas this afternoon.

Things were happening so fast that it seemed to be more like a dream than reality. After a short time, we had my car packed with her personal items and were on the road. She was paid up for two more weeks on her trailer, and we'd have to come back to get her car and a few more non-necessity items. She didn't want to take her car at this time because she said the "check engine" light was staying on and she needed to have it checked before she drove it on a long trip. This time, we made the trip without incident, and Janet and Dad made her feel very welcome. She was given the girls' bedroom, and after we got her settled in, I walked her around the farm. We strolled out to the barn where I told her about several of my boyhood memories.

Then we made it down to the pond and eventually through the woods and to the creek. While walking along the creek just before Christmas, I told her the stories I remembered hearing about how Uncle Ben romanced Aunt Mary Ann on a similar creek about seventy-five or so years ago. She said it was a very romantic setting, and she could see how romance could be kindled in such a place. Then she turned and looked at me face to face and said again, "Richard, I love you and don't want you to ever be gone from my life. I can't even imagine having a family as wonderful as yours who will just take me in as if I am part of the family. I will never forget this kindness."

A lump came up in my throat, and I wanted to tell her that I loved her too, but the words just wouldn't come out. Instead, I kissed her and embraced her with a tight hug. Soon, we were back at the house because it was getting cold and the fire in the fireplace sounded pretty good to both of us. Janet had some hot chocolate ready for us, which I must admit hit the spot better than hot, black coffee.

As we sat and drank our chocolate, Dad told her about our tradition of cutting down a tree each year a few weeks before Christmas. I suggested that tomorrow Talisa and I go find one and cut it and bring it back to the house for decorating. She seemed excited to do so as she said she had always put up an artificial tree. Dad also began telling her a little bit about the job he had lined out for her which was mostly clerical work and answering the phone.

Since I was on medical leave until January 1, I decided to stay in East Texas and spend more time with Talisa. While there, Dad and I discussed more the Hopes Landing project, and Talisa was becoming an asset at the office. Every day after work and before dark, which wasn't very much time, I'd drive Talisa around and show her some of my favorite boyhood sites.

One afternoon, we drove by the orphanage that Uncle Ben and Aunt Mary Ann had started. I told her that my Uncle Ben had become a legend in this community. His death earlier in the year marked a sad day for many and he was greatly missed. We stopped, and I introduced her to Aunt Mary Ann, who was almost ninety-two but still just as sharp as a tack. As soon as we walked into her house, she wanted to know if we had time for a piece of cake and coffee. We declined as it was almost time for supper.

Later that night, Talisa and I were sitting on the front porch snuggled in the porch swing and covered with a blanket. Although the night air was crisp, it was not freezing cold like previous December nights that I remembered. While swinging and talking, Talisa asked me about the Hopes Landing Project. I was taken aback for a moment and finally asked her why she asked that. She said she had overheard the conversation about it in the office and occasionally my name was included in the talk. She was just curious about what everyone was talking about.

Well, I wrestled within myself - should I or should I not tell her? Finally, I told her there was a corrupt town called "Hopes

Landing," and we were putting together a plan to try to expose the corruption and hopefully clean up the town.

Naturally, this raised other questions like ' how and when'. I felt very uneasy about divulging too much information as I still didn't trust her 100 percent especially after she had kept her felony a secret from me. I couldn't really see how she could be a plant for Sheriff Hagan, but stranger things have happened. So to her questions, I said the details haven't been worked out yet. Soon, the subject changed to the beautiful full moon, which was fine with me.

The next morning, Dad asked me to come by his office, and when I got there, a young black man I'd guess to be in his mid-twenties was also there. Dad introduced him to me as Taylor. He said Taylor was the FBI agent who would be going to Hopes Landing with me. In addition, Taylor had brought some of the reconnaissance rings for me to try on for size. I picked one that fit after which we discussed our mission. Dad and Taylor were talking about different signal frequencies that could be used, which was over my head. After Taylor left, Dad said, "Son, things are falling nicely into place, but for now, let's shut it down for Christmas."

As we walked out of the office, Talisa commented how neat it was that the merchants in town had decorated so much for Christmas. All the stores had some type of Christmas display while the buildings were all outlined with white Christmas lights. As we walked to the car, she began to sing, "It's beginning to look a lot like Christmas."

This year, in keeping with family tradition, we were all to meet at Grandpa Pete and Granny Jean's for Christmas dinner, but it would not be the same as years past because Uncle Ben would not be there to tell us one of his intriguing stories. Perhaps, Grandpa Pete will pick up the tradition and tell us some basketball stories that he remembers from his Boston Celtic days.

7
Chapter

Christmas Eve had arrived, and Talisa kept expressing how much she had fallen in love with my family and was looking forward to tomorrow when she would be able to meet more of the people that I had talked so much about. Finally, my curiosity got the best of me, and I asked about her family.

She said that she really had no family. While growing up she was pretty close to a younger brother, but when she got into trouble with the law and went to prison, her family felt ashamed and wrote her a letter which basically said they were disowning her as a daughter, and as far as they were concerned, she was dead and that there was to be no more contact of any kind between them. Her eyes began to water, and her lower lip started to tremble as she said, "So you see, I have no place to go. For the past several years, I have always volunteered to work on holidays which helped ease the hurt and loneliness."

I could not imagine such and told her that I was so sorry but was glad she was with me and my family this year. She said she was glad too and hoped this would not be the last time. Again, I wasn't sure how to respond to that, so I said nothing for a few seconds before mumbling, "Me too."

Later that night, she and Janet were baking for Christmas Dinner that would be at Grandpa Pete's. Dad and I were watching Texas and Arkansas play football on television, but I could over-hear their conversation in the kitchen. Talisa asked Janet how long it took her to fit in and feel a part of this family. Janet said she felt that she belonged immediately as everyone reached out to her and made her feel welcome. She continued to say that after she and Dad were engaged, she felt like she had always been a member of the family. Talisa said, "I hope I can feel the same someday."

"Maybe you will," Janet replied.

Was I being selfish, or cautious, by not sharing my true feelings with Talisa? Was I being any different than she by keeping things from her? I think my problem was partly because I wasn't sure I knew what romantic love was. I had strong feelings for her and enjoyed her company, but is that love? I wasn't sure. I had never been in love with a woman before.

Later that evening, after the football game was over and the baking was finished, I asked Talisa to go for a walk with me. Naturally she was glad to do so. It was a crisp evening with the temperature in the high thirties, so a warm coat felt really good. The night was a romantic one as the moon was almost full and the sky was filled with twinkling stars. We went to the barn and sat on square bales of hay as we looked into the sky for falling stars.

I knew deep inside of me that this was the time for me to tell Talisa how I felt. I had bought her a ring for Christmas, although it was not an engagement ring. I had it in my pocket and wanted to give it to her. Even though it was near freezing and vapor that looked like smoke was coming from our mouths as we spoke, I was having a hot flash and felt like I was about to smother. Why was I feeling this way?

Eventually, I mustered up the courage and said, "Talisa, I have something I want to give you as a Christmas gift. It's not much and not wrapped either, but it's from my heart." Then I gave her the ring that was set with her birthstone. I wish I could have captured the expression of happiness on her face.

"Oh, Richard! I have never been given anything more meaningful than this! Thank you. I love you." Then she came into my arms and gave me a passionate kiss like I had never experienced before.

"Talisa, can we talk for a moment?"

"Sure. I thought that's what we have been doing."

"No. I mean seriously." Then I somehow found the words to say. "Talisa, listen to me very carefully. Several times in several different ways you have told me that you loved me, but I have never returned the sentiment. I don't know why I haven't. I know I care about you, and I don't want to be away from you, but I'm afraid of falling in love. I saw what happened to my mom and dad when they went through their divorce. I was just a kid, but it made me afraid to make any kind of commitment. Even though they eventually got back together, the emotional scar stayed with me. For a long time, I couldn't put my finger on the reason why I couldn't tell you that I love you. But tonight, it came to me that I was just afraid to fall in love. Now, I have just finally realized that my feelings outweigh my fears. Talisa, I love you, and I want this ring to be a promise ring from me to you. Tonight, I am promising my love and allegiance to you and only you."

"Oh, Richard! I've never heard anything sweeter. You don't know how I've longed to hear those words from you, and they are all the more meaningful because I know it is not some come-on line with you. While I don't have a ring to give you, I promise my love to you just the same."

We continued sitting on the hay bales and talking. I felt a burden had been lifted off my chest and now the words came easy as we continued to freely share our feelings and apprehensions. As the evening came to a close, I told her that I was looking forward to showing her off tomorrow. She smiled and said she was looking forward to showing off her ring.

That night, I still wondered if I had done the right thing, but soon my wondering turned into sleep.

The next morning, we were all up early and getting ready for Christmas Dinner. About nine, Paige, Tiffany, and Darrin arrived, and as usual, the last one to show up was my sister Rachael. She was always late. I remember Dad saying once that Rachael would be late to her own funeral. As each arrived, there were hugs and laughter. The kids immediately headed to the barn. It seems the hay was always a big hit for them, and after they left, Dad always had to go out and restack some of the bales that got tumbled, but he never seemed to mind.

Finally, about noon, we all made our way over to Grandpa Pete's. When we arrived, most all the gang was there, and Talisa was astounded at how big the crowd was. Without counting, I'd guess around fifty or so were standing out in the yard and on the porch, and as I expected, they all made Talisa feel very welcome. It would also be a sad day in one respect because we no longer had Uncle Ben with us.

Unlike some other Christmases, the weather was beautiful, and after eating, the children could stay outside and play while the grown-ups watched college football on TV. The women who didn't care about football gathered around the kitchen table and talked. Talisa watched some football with me but then made her way to the kitchen. As we watched the game, I told the others that they needed to keep up with LSU next year as a kid named Logan was going to make a name for himself playing for us.

Sometime during the third quarter, I heard a flood of comments coming from the kitchen like, "Oh, it's beautiful!" and "I'm so excited for you two!" I knew the women were talking about Talisa's ring and she had told them it was a promise ring. Deep down I was proud.

Soon, Christmas was over and all the family made their way back to their respective homes. Dad had a couple of cheating-husband cases to investigate, and it was time for me to get back to Baton Rouge. I knew as long as Talisa was in East Texas that I'd be making frequent visits even though it was a seven-hour drive as compared to three hours to see her at Lake Charles.

On January 2, I was in the LSU coach's office watching video clips of all the new recruits. Coach Bevels wanted me to study the players and help him build a new offense that was centered around Logan. He liked my ideas and said it would be so exciting to have Logan on the team.

Eventually, the conversation got around to the release form that must be signed by Logan's mother. Being backed into a corner, I felt compelled to tell Coach Bevels about our plans so he would know why it would be a while longer before I could get the paper.

During the next few weeks, I made a visit to see Logan and several visits to east Texas. Then one morning I got a call from Dad while I had gone out for some donuts. He left a message that said, "Richard, it's time. We'll be at your place first thing in the morning." I can't explain the way I felt. On one hand, I was excited, but on the other hand, I was scared to death. After hearing the message, I lost my appetite and couldn't eat the warm, good-smelling donuts. The rest of the day I did nothing but lie around, which made me feel worse, and needless to say, I slept very little that night.

About six-thirty the next morning, Dad was knocking on my door. I let him in along with Taylor and several other agents. They no doubt had driven most of the night to arrive so early. We had a briefing in my living room before we headed out. I was given a ring that had a small, concealed microphone in it while Taylor had one with a camera lens. The plan was for me and Taylor to go into town and make myself known first at the café, and if that didn't alert the sheriff and his deputies, I was to go to the school. Between the two, I should be picked up by a sheriff's deputy as I had been warned not to come back to their town. There would be two vans parked separately in the grocery store parking lot. One had the appearance of a plumbing van from Donaldsonville, and the other appeared to be a boat repair service. In addition, a couple of cars would be stationed just a few miles outside the town.

Taylor was to pretend to be one of the coaches from LSU. We were to arrive shortly after the vans were in place. Before we left, the agents replaced my car radio with one that had a receiving channel where I could hear their conversations. They also replaced my state inspection sticker with one that was out of date. Finally, all was set, and it was time to go. My heart was about to pound out of my body! Dad led us in prayer and then we were off.

It took about an hour and a half to drive from Baton Rouge to Hope's Landing, and there was very little talking between Taylor and me. I did find out that he had played football for a small college in Alabama, so the role of a coach was not completely foreign to him. I also found out that he was married and had an eighteen-month-old baby girl and another one due in three months. He had a lot more at stake than I did.

We were getting close to town when we heard over my car radio, "We just got into town and stopped by the grocery store for some bottled water before going to the job site. Van 1 is in place and ready." Soon we got a similar message about Van 2 as we were passing by the city limits sign.

As we were pulling in front of the café, I told the others over the radio where we were and asked if they could hear me, and I got a "ten-four" in response. I changed the radio station to a country music channel before turning it off. Taylor and I made our way inside the café and took a seat at a booth near the window. A different waitress from last time took our order, but I introduced myself and Taylor to her and was bragging to Taylor in front of her about what a good breakfast this place served. I told him when I was here before on a recruiting trip that I ate here. I was hoping that would be enough bait to set the trap.

Sure enough, as we were almost finished eating, my favorite obnoxious deputy drove up. He apparently recognized my car and gave it a good looking over before coming into the café. After a few minutes, he walked in and immediately came over to our table. "Well, Mr. Scroggins, I'm surprised to see you here. I see you have some company with you."

"Hello, Deputy. This is Coach Hudson, and we are still looking for some football players. Any law against that?" I asked.

"Nah. No law against that, but the inspection sticker on your car has expired, and there is a law against that. Scroggins, you and Hudson need to come with me."

I balked and told him, "No, I'm not going with you. You can write me a ticket for having an inspection sticker overdue, but I don't need to go with you anywhere."

I could see his face getting red as he immediately radioed for backup. "We have Scroggins at Rose's, and he is refusing arrest. Need backup to restrain him."

As he was talking on the radio, Taylor stood up, and immediately the deputy went for his gun. Taylor decked him with a strong right punch. "Come on! Let's go!" he shouted. As we rushed out the front door, three other deputy cars pulled up and we surrendered to them. By this time, the deputy walked out of the café, and as he did, the other deputies held Taylor while the bully worked him over pretty good before tossing him into the patrol car. They put me in a different car, but I knew we were both headed to see Sheriff Hagan. Within a few minutes, we were standing in the sheriff's office. "Well, Scroggins, you just couldn't stay away from our town, could ya? Well, this time it will probably cost you. Now, your friend here has to learn that it doesn't pay to hang out with you, and it certainly doesn't pay to cross me in my town." Then he took his cane and poked Taylor in the stomach before rapping him across the face.

I figured this was my cue, so I began by saying, "Alright, Hagan, we all know this is your town and you are the tough guy. All we want is football players, but it seems some of them have disappeared in the swamps at your orders. How many people have you killed?"

"Scroggins, that's enough out of you! Your mouth is about to get you in deeper trouble than you want to be."

"What's wrong, Hagan? Does the truth hurt? You're a tough man when you have all these deputies to do your dirty work for you. Just how many have you buried in the swamps? I imagine at least a dozen. Am I right?" I could tell he was getting hot under the collar. "It doesn't matter how many because I'm going to add two more!" he shouted back.

"Who? Us? Just a couple of football recruiters? Come on, Hagan. You know we are no threat to you and your illegal gator poaching." I knew by his facial expression that I had really hit a nerve this time.

"You didn't know I knew that, did ya? If a mere football recruiter can figure that out, how long do you think it will be before the feds figure out what's going on down here and swarm this place if I come up missing? Come on, Hagan, wise up. Let me get my football players and I'll leave."

"Scroggins, I have a better idea. You are like a fly in that you are annoying me. I swat a fly to get rid of him, but you will have to swim the swamp with chains on." When he said that, his deputies grabbed both Taylor and me, and within a matter of seconds, we were both bound with chains around our feet and hands.

"Is this how you do it, Hagan? You tie 'em up with chains and then toss 'em into the swamp?"

"That always seems to work pretty good. We'll see how well you two can swim with weights on," Hagan said.

"Alright, Hagan, it looks like this is the end for me, but let Coach Hudson go. He has caused you no problem, and he has a wife and children at home waiting for him."

"You know I can't do that. He knows too much, and besides, he publically assaulted an officer of the law. And just for your peace of mind, we have probably gotten rid of at least twenty people just like you that crossed us - but we are still here, and they became gator bait."

I hoped that was enough recorded testimony, and I was expecting the FBI agents to come busting in through the door at any time, but instead, a dispatcher rushed in and said, "Sir, we have a strange radio frequency being transmitted from this building. I don't know what it is."

Hagan looked at me with fire in his eyes and said, "I think I do."

8

Chapter

Hagan walked toward me, and naturally, my heart was about to beat out of my chest. When he got right in front of me, he said, "Where's the wire?"

I assured him that I didn't have a wire. He ordered a strip search of both Taylor and me, and of course, they found no wire. While standing before them naked, he ordered all our jewelry to be removed. They collected a necklace that Taylor was wearing, wrist watches that each of us had, plus our rings. They tossed the rings and necklace into a basket but closely examined the watches. With all our stuff removed, the dispatcher came back in and told Sheriff Hagan that the signal was still being transmitted, and he finally concluded it was coming from somewhere else rather than from us. After all, we were standing before him completely exposed and nothing was attached to us.

We were allowed to get dressed, and as we were doing so, a deputy reported that a suspicious-looking van was in the grocery store parking lot. Immediately, Hagan rushed Taylor and me into a police car and raced to the dock. We left in such a hurry that the rings were left behind in the plastic container. I hoped the FBI agents had recorded enough dialog, but I wished I was still wearing the ring. I also hoped that Taylor's ring had sent some good pictures.

As we were being forced into a boat with Hagen and some deputies, the FBI agents were closing in. When we were a few hundred yards out into the water, I could see the agents rushing across the dock and the deputies raising their hands into the air, but we were already out into the water and racing down the bayou. We were soon out of sight of the dock and the agents. Hagan was so angry that I believe he could have bitten a nail in two.

When we were out in the middle of a swampy area, Hagan stopped the boat. As he did, he asked me again who I worked for. I told him again that I worked as a sports recruiter for LSU, but because of the way he had treated me before, I was cooperating with the FBI to break up his corrupt stronghold on this community. He pulled out his gun and said that he might go down but neither Taylor nor I would be alive to see it. Then he asked Taylor if he was an agent. Taylor kept silent. This made the sheriff all the angrier. He asked him again, and again Taylor uttered not a word.

Then without warning, Hagen shot Taylor right in the chest! Taylor slumped and moaned. I reached over to help him, but the deputies pushed me aside and then tossed him over the edge of the boat. I knew that I was to be next, so I jumped out of the boat into the murky water. The weight of the chains around my hands was pulling me down, but while underneath the boat, I had enough strength in my legs to kick my way through the water to the bow of the boat. Since it was a flat-bottom John Boat, it was sloped in the front which gave me a place to surface while shielded by the bow of the boat. As I swam, I noticed a piece of rope dangling from the boat that was used to tie it to the dock. I grabbed hold of the rope which kept me from sinking to the bottom of the swamp.

I feared for Taylor, but right now I couldn't think about him. I knew that I couldn't hang onto the boat rope when they started back to the dock. I needed to find something else to hang on to. After a few minutes, I heard Hagan say, "Well, I guess Scroggins is gator bait too as I don't see him anywhere. We might as well head to Port Ida. There shouldn't be any Feds there, and we'll meet some of our clients who can fly us to Mexico."

They revved up the motor, and as the boat picked up speed, I knew I couldn't hang on to the rope much longer and especially with my arms in the chains. I also knew if I turned loose now that most likely I'd be hit by the propeller before I could get out of the way. But I had no choice.

I took a deep breath and let go of the rope and the weight of the chains pulled me deep into the water quickly, but not quick enough to avoid the prop. It hit my left arm as I was trying to stay in an upright position. The pain was excruciating, but nonetheless, I kicked with all the strength I could muster and finally reached the surface where I took a much-needed breath of air. But soon fatigue set in, and I began to sink once more. I kept kicking and floundering in the water. Hagan and his crew were now several hundred yards down the bayou, so I wasn't too worried about being seen by them. My first concern was to try to get to a cypress tree where I could climb upon its root mass, and secondly, I must somehow stop the bleeding of my arm. If only I didn't have those chains on my arms! Holding my hands upward, I frantically kicked my legs just to stay afloat. There were many trees in the swamp on either side of the boat channel, but they were a good distance away, and I wasn't sure I could make it. The water around me was now turning red with my blood. My only hope was to try to swim.

I spotted the closest tree, and with my arms held upward toward heaven, I rolled over on my back and headed toward it with a prayer on my lips. My arms and legs were both getting tired, but I had to keep going if I was to live. Finally, I could go no farther. My loss of blood had weakened me, and my legs just quit. When I quit kicking, I began to sink. As I was sinking, I had a flashback of my dreams in the hospital. Oddly enough, I felt calm as I realized those dreams were coming true. This was the end.

Soon, I hit bottom, and when I did, I immediately gathered my legs below me and pushed off the bottom. As I stood and pushed, I realized that the water was only a few feet over my head, and with very little effort, I could push upward to the surface. As I surfaced, I took a large breath of air before going back under the water. Again I pushed upward for another breath of air. I'm sure I looked like a bobber in the water, but I was able to maintain the bobbing effort until I reached the trees. When I reached the root base of the trees, which protruded several feet under the water from the trunk, I struggled but finally was able to crawl up onto the tree base and out of the water. I must confess, breathing air had never felt so good. I thanked God for keeping me alive.

Now I was faced with the problem of getting the chains off and the bleeding stopped. I tried to reach around to my cut and found that I could reach it. So I crawled around on the tree until I found some gray Spanish moss that I could reach and also found a little bit of mud in the crevice of the tree roots. I pulled off some of the moss and covered it with mud and placed it over my cut. It seemed to be working as the blood stopped dripping on the roots and in the water that was around me. But like swimming in the water, I knew I couldn't hold the packing very long. I had to find some other way to secure it to my arm.

I held the patch against my arm and then leaned up against the tree trunk to hold it in place. This seemed to work which freed my hands. I needed to get free from the chains that were actually attached to handcuffs. I pulled and pried but to no avail. I lubricated my hands with mud in an attempt to slip them through the handcuffs, but that didn't work either. My arm was hurting, but I had stopped the bleeding which was a good thing. I just sat on the tree roots that were above the water.

The day passed slowly as I sat in the sun and watched nature all around me. Had it been under different circumstances, I would have really enjoyed this setting but now I was concerned about staying alive.

I wondered if arrests had been made and if Sheriff Hagan was caught before he could leave for Mexico. I felt bad about the news waiting to be told to Taylor's family. I wished I could see Talisa, and I wondered if I would ever see her again. I knew I had to get out of the swamp, but I couldn't swim. After dark, I could easily become a meal for some swamp predator, but what was I to do? I figured my best hope was to sit tight and hope a boat might come by. I waited and watched and fatigue finally overtook me. I fell asleep in the afternoon sun with a prayer in my heart and on my lips.

Late in the day, I was awakened by a person shaking me. I was startled at first fearing Sheriff Hagan had returned, but I soon figured out it was another man with two young boys who I presumed were his sons. He introduced himself as Roscoe while he was trying to help me into his Cajun pirogue. He introduced me to his sons that he called Pepe and Alex. Once I was inside the pirogue, the boys used push-poles to navigate us through the swamp. After what I'd guess to be about thirty minutes, we stopped in front of a river shack. Roscoe helped me ashore and into the house. I didn't know solid ground could ever feel so good. Once inside, Roscoe introduced me to his wife and what appeared to be a teenage daughter.

"Looks like you met Sheriff Hagan," Roscoe said. I nodded that I had. Roscoe left me with his wife, and she tended to my arm and dressed it with some kind of grease-looking stuff. I guess I looked concerned, so she said, "Alligator fat. It is great for wounds." I had a hard time understanding either of them because they talked with a strong Cajun accent.

After she finished treating my arm, Roscoe came in with some bolt cutters and freed my hands from the handcuffs and chains. What a relief this was, and what a blessing he was!

Later, after they fed me some kind of gumbo, he told me that he and his family were called "swamp rats." He said years ago he lived in New Orleans and worked for the police department there, but he became so disgruntled with mankind that he decided to escape into the swamps and live a life in seclusion. He has raised his family here and they lived on their survival skills. He said he had not been in civilization in over ten years.

I was enthralled by his story. He was certainly no dummy. He would have to be pretty sharp to be able to survive the way he had. That night they bedded me down in a small hut on a cot made of stretched deer hide. I was amazed at how comfortable it was. Before I fell asleep, I wondered how I was going to get out of this swamp. I hoped I could get him to take me but wondered if he expected me to spend the rest of my life like him and become a "swamp rat." I certainly had no answers, but I knew time would tell. For now, I was dry, safe, and alive for which I was thankful.

For the next several days, I lay around the fishing camp as my body healed. I watched in amazement at the way this family lived. Each person had a role to play and the family unit functioned like a well-oiled machine. The more I watched, the more I considered the benefits of their lifestyle. They left others alone, and they were left alone. They were at peace and enjoyed life without all the worldly pressures. I assumed the kids had never even heard of a TV or a computer.

What really impressed me more than everything else was their spiritual values. The children respected and obeyed their parents without any rebellion or sass. Every morning, they gathered for breakfast, and Roscoe read a chapter from the Bible. Then they did the same thing at the evening meal. I was beginning to think Roscoe had life figured out.

A week passed and I was slowly re-gaining the use of my arm. Roscoe informed me that he wanted me to go with him into the swamp the next day. Naturally, I agreed and was excited to go see what he does, but I was a little apprehensive as well. I asked him what we would do if we ran into Sheriff Hagan. He simply smiled and said, "We won't." That was good enough for me.

That night I couldn't go to sleep and my mind began to wonder. I again wondered if the sheriff had made it into Mexico. If he did, how were things running back in Hopes Landing? I knew Dad was concerned about me and that he figured I was no longer alive. I also wondered about Talisa and how she was taking the news of "my death". I assumed the agents had all left the area and gone back to their respective homes. I was so sorry Taylor had been killed and no doubt eaten by the gators. I wondered why I had ever gotten so involved in the life of Logan anyway. It certainly hadn't been worth all of the pain it had caused. So what if LSU didn't have the best football team in the area? All of that seemed so trivial to me now.

The next morning after breakfast, Roscoe and I pushed off in his pirogue. I was in the front as he skillfully maneuvered us through the swamp from sitting in the back. After a bit, we slowly made our way up to a debris drift. He instructed me to reach over the front of the boat and grab the rope that was attached to the tree root. I looked and finally spotted the rope just a few inches below the water's surface. I grabbed the rope and began to try to pull it in, but I realized that it was not only hard to pull, but that it was active. Something alive was on the other end! I looked back at Roscoe with eyes of apprehension and fear. He assured me it was alright, so I kept pulling. Soon, I had a fish trap near the boat, and I could tell that there were at least six large catfish in the box, maybe more. Again, I looked back to Roscoe for instructions, and he motioned for me to pull the fish out of the cage and put them on a stringer that he had. After the fish were on the stringer, we hung them in the water outside the pirogue to keep them alive. There were eight of them that probably weighed six to ten pounds each. He then tossed me some kind of meat to put inside the trap for bait. I did that and lowered it back into the water.

Then we left and headed to what I presumed to be another trap. I noticed Roscoe did not talk while we were on the water. Instead, his eyes and ears were constantly in tune with our surroundings. After we had traveled up the channel, he stopped and said to me, "Hear that?" I listened and heard the sound of a motorboat. With precision, he pushed us out of the boat channel and into the wooded swamp where we quietly sat. Soon, the boat passed us by. It had what looked to be two fishermen in it. When it was out of sight, Roscoe pushed us back out into the channel. "You see, Sheriff Hagan would never find you." Now I understood why.

We got back to the camp a little past noon and had thirty-three fish for Alex and Pepe to clean. Later that afternoon, some visitors came and traded some supplies for the fish. When they left, Roscoe said they were his contacts for getting supplies that he needed.

For several weeks, this was my routine. I asked him repeatedly if he would take me to a place where I could return to my own life and where I could contact my family to let them know I was alive. He always said no to my request. I wasn't in any kind of danger, but I was beginning to think the control he had over me was much like the control Sheriff Hagen had over the people in Hopes Landing. Once more, I wondered if he was still there, or if the FBI agents had made sure he never returned.

I also continued to wonder about my family and Talisa and wondered if perhaps Taylor was still alive like me, or if his body had been recovered. I assumed the gators ate every part of the body and there was nothing to recover. I also assumed he had no chance of surviving after the gunshot and with the chains around his hands. Somehow, I needed to get word to Dad that I was alive, but I didn't even know where I was. If I were to try to escape to freedom, I didn't know which way to go. I could tell from the sun which way was north, but was that the best way out of here? Perhaps east or west would be closer to civilization.

One day, we had a conversation, and I again asked Roscoe to take me to a place where I could find my way out of the swamps. His answer to that was that he had really expected me to die, but since I had lived, he wanted me to stay with them and become a husband to his daughter. I tried to explain to him that I had a woman already and that I needed to get back to her. His reply was, "They think you are dead. By now they have given up on your return, so there should be no problem with you staying here forever and becoming my son-in-law." One day it was raining and Roscoe decided that we should stay inside. Usually, we were out in the swamp rain or shine, but today was different. I began trying to think of a way I could escape. I had lost track of time, but I figured I had been here at least a couple of months and perhaps longer. I had a full beard and dirty shoulder-length hair. I only had one set of clothes which were really soiled. Roscoe occasionally loaned me some of his clothes long enough for me to wash mine in the dirty swampy water, but his were really uncomfortable because they were too small for me. If I managed to escape, people would probably be afraid of me because of my appearance.

That night I really got homesick and re-played in my mind the evening before Christmas with Talisa. Oh, how I missed her, and now more than ever, I knew that I was in love with her. I regretted the thought that she was grieving and mourning my death, but it was so close to being true. I knew that I would always be grateful to Roscoe for saving my life, but I also knew I couldn't live the rest of my life here in the swamps nor could I marry his young daughter. How could I legally marry her anyway with no marriage license or no one to perform the ceremony, etc., but I guess none of that would be important to Roscoe or his family. I couldn't imagine me having children with her and raising them here without them ever being able to go to school or see any of the world and its beauty.

I decided I needed to befriend some of the traders who come to the camp and try to get them to take me out of here. I didn't want to be a "swamp-rat"! But planning that would take some time. If only I still had the ring, Dad and others could pick up my messages and eventually find me. At the least, they would know I was alive and well, but I didn't have it.

I wondered if I could get some paper and pen and write a letter to let the family know that I was alive. Perhaps, I could smuggle it out with the traders, or maybe Roscoe would let me send it without having to sneak it out. It would be worth mentioning tomorrow.

The next day after our morning breakfast and devotional, while gathering the few things that we needed to go out into the swamp, I asked Roscoe about writing a letter to my folks back home. He stopped what he was doing and walked over near me and looked me in the eye and said, "This is your home now and we are your folks – we don't need a letter." Then he returned to what he was doing. Once again, I wondered if I was any better off than the people living in Hopes Landing I knew from Roscoe's answer that I needed to consider some other method of getting out of here. Maybe I could take the pirogue late one night and slip away, but that would leave Roscoe and his family helpless and might even lead to their deaths as they depended on that boat for their survival.

Maybe I could convince him to build a second pirogue, then I could slip out and not cause any harm to them. After all, they saved my life, and in a way, they have been very good to me. They have treated me like one of their family, but the problem is that I don't want to be part of their family!

There was always the option of trying to swim/wade out of the swamp. Over the past several weeks I had learned a great deal about the swamp and the inhabitants of it. Most everyone thinks the alligators are the worst predators in the water, but they are not nearly as dangerous or deadly as coral snakes. I also learned that most of the swamp is relatively shallow, less than three or four feet except for the boat channels, which might be ten feet or more. So if need be, I could literally walk out of the majority of the swamp if it were not for the soggy mud bottom. But which direction would I go?

Also during the past few weeks, I had become pretty good at skinning fish and small swamp animals, particularly swamp rabbits. There were parts of the swamp where the water was only a few inches deep with spots of dry land protruding. This was a paradise for small animals and waterfowl. It was in these places that Roscoe had snares set and was very successful at trapping. He willingly shared his skills with me as he was considering me to be his son-in-law.

As the weeks passed, I tried to learn as much as I could about survival in the swamps. I became proficient with a bow and arrow and a hunting knife which I made. I learned how to fish and trap. I knew a lot, but I still didn't know the way out!

One day I suggested to Roscoe that we build another pirogue that would allow us to go in separate directions and double our yield. He thought about that idea for a while and finally said he didn't like it. He said we were already getting enough food to survive and anything more would spoil. "It's like the manna was to the children of God as they wandered in the wilderness. One day's supply was sufficient. No, Richard, we don't need another pirogue. Besides, if we had another one, you might be tempted to leave us."

9

Chapter

I had no idea how long I had been in the swamps, but the weather was getting very hot, so I assumed it was summertime. I had seen no newspaper, no TV, or had any contact with the outside world since I had been here. More and more I was beginning to feel like I was a prisoner. I was still grateful that Roscoe had saved my life, and I was thankful for a place to live and food to eat, yet I had such a deep gnawing inside of me that I had to get out of here.

I wasn't sleeping well at night. I kept thinking about Taylor's family and the two small children who would grow up without their dad, and I realized it was completely my fault that he was killed. I knew the risk I was taking when I went back into Hopes Landing, and now I couldn't imagine why I would have put my own life and the lives of others in danger just to get Logan to play football for LSU. I missed my family, and I especially missed Talisa. I wondered if she still wore my promise ring, or if by now she had found a new boyfriend. I knew my family thought I was dead, and that they would all be grieving. I so wished I knew how to let them know that I was alive. I figured the university had found a replacement for me as a recruiter and that I no longer had a job there.

The more I thought about it, the more I decided I was going to attempt to walk out, and I figured my clue as to the direction to go was going to have to come from the traders. First, I had to befriend them and gain their trust, and then maybe I could get some information out of them.

In a couple of days, an older man arrived who traded cooking supplies for fish. Roscoe always met and negotiated with the traders, but this time I made a point to meander over. I didn't do anything but speak and stand in the background. They spoke Cajun talk, so I had a hard time understanding what they were saying, but I noticed that the old man kept glancing my way as if he wasn't too sure about my presence. Soon the transaction was over, and he left. As he was leaving, I waved and he waved back as he was easing his boat out into the channel.

After he left, I told Roscoe that I'd like to learn a little bit about the business end of this life, and he said he would show me when the time was right. It seems that every time I have a scheme in mind, Roscoe either figured it out, or else he was very shrewd. Perhaps, it is a little of both. But I knew from his comment that I would not be allowed to get close to the traders for a long time.

That night I tried to remember the geography of southern Louisiana. I knew from driving down Interstate 10 between Lafayette and Baton Rouge that the Atchafalaya River Basin was much longer than it was wide, and it had a width of about twenty miles. That meant my walk out would most likely have to be either east or west because the basin was probably well over a hundred miles to the north. Then again, New Iberia shouldn't be all that far to the south. I knew where Hopes Landing was with respect to Morgan City, which made me think that perhaps, going east would be my best route. After I pondered all these things, I finally decided east would be my best choice. After all, it was from there that we came here by boat, and the trip didn't seem to take us very long. I knew also that if I kept going east, I would eventually hit the highway between Hopes Landing and Morgan City. The biggest danger, aside from gators and snakes, is going around in circles as you are prone to do when you can't see your direction clearly.

The next morning, as we were getting ready to go out and check our traps, I asked Roscoe what he knew about Sheriff

Hagan. He said that from the cover of the swamp, he had personally seen Sheriff Hagan execute and toss at least a half-dozen men into the water. He said he is a very ruthless man.

As he was saying that I was thinking 'eye-witness testimony'. So I continued to probe. "Have you ever met him personally, and does he know you live back here?"

"No, I've never met him, and I don't know if he knows I'm here or not. I have never seen his boat back in here. We are a little too deep into the swamp for his interest," Roscoe said. Naturally, I tuned in on the ' a little too deep into the swamp' comment.

"So he never comes up this boat channel?" I quizzed.

"As far as I know, he hasn't. His channel and dumping ground is the next channel over." He was pointing to the east as he was talking.

"Is that where you found me?"

"Yeah. I was looking for another place to set traps when we saw you lying up on that tree."

Then I said, "Roscoe, this may seem crazy, but Hagan shot my friend that day and tossed him into the water. Do you think you could take me back there just on the off chance I might find some of his remains? That would mean the world to me."

He stood silently as he loaded the last set of cages into the boat. I wasn't sure he had heard me. Finally, he broke his silence by saying, "As long as it's been, there ain't nothing left of your friend." I took that as a "no."

But from that conversation, I learned that there was another boating channel to the east and most likely it was the one that leads to Hopes Landing. I figured it must not be too far away since Roscoe was considering setting some traps over there. I now knew most definitely that I should go to the east when I decide to leave.

We pushed off to go check the traps in hopes of having some game with a market value. By now I had become like Roscoe in that I didn't talk but listened and watched as we maneuvered through the swamp and its channels. Occasionally, we would hear motorboats and would conceal ourselves until they passed.

I also had learned much about the animals of the swamp, particularly alligators. Almost every time we went out, I would spot two or three and sometimes more. When I saw them, they were usually lying on top of something basking in the sun. Roscoe told me that they sunned most of the day and did their feeding at night because their prey was sleeping and easier to catch.

On this particular day, I was paying more attention to my surroundings with the idea of escape in my mind. I was trying to mentally map out the places where the high ground was and where other channels crossed. Unless you are extremely familiar with the swamp, it all looks the same, and all the boat channels definitely look the same. So I was trying to establish some landmarks as we pushed along from one channel into another one.

Finally, we pushed up to a tree to check a fish trap instead of an animal trap. We had been here several times before while checking fish traps, and I thought it was a little odd to be checking a fish trap while our mission was to be checking animal traps. But I pulled up the trap and unloaded three catfish. Just before we pushed away, and to my amazement, Roscoe said, "Richard, I want you to look around and see if you see anything that belongs to your friend. You see, this is the tree where I found you."

I was shocked! I had been here quite a few times before, but I had no inkling that this was where I was when Roscoe found me. Like I said, all the swamp looks alike. Although I was paying close attention, I still wasn't sure I could come here without Roscoe's help, and I also wondered if he was telling me the truth. Nevertheless, I planned to pay closer attention on our way back to camp. I needed to learn my way to get back here. Before we left, I noticed a particular cypress tree with a root mass that looked like a horse head plus it had a broken limb toward the top that made it look different from all the others around it. That could be my landmark.

We followed the channel northward until we came to the first crossing channel. We turned left and went west for what seemed to be a mile or so before we turned left again at the next crossing channel which took us back to our cottage. So the best

I could calculate, I should be able to wade the swamp eastward for a couple of miles and intersect the channel that Hagan used with Taylor and me.

I decided to wait a few more days before making my move for a couple of reasons. One was to perhaps divert my intentions and secondly to improve my geography knowledge. I would use these days to make mental notes of unique landmarks along the channels.

Finally, I felt it was time to make my move. I planned to slip out in the middle of the night and swim across the boat channel until I got to the shallow water. From there, I could wade into the wooded swamp just a short distance where I would climb out of the water and wait until daylight. I wanted to be far enough into the cover so as not to be detected by Roscoe and his family, but not so far that I would run the risk of being attacked by a gator while it was dark. Finally, after everyone seemed to be asleep, I quietly got up and strapped on my hunting knife, picked up my bow and several arrows which I tucked inside my belt, and eased out of camp toward the canal. As I got near the water's edge, I heard something behind me and turned only to see Roscoe walking outside! I immediately hunkered down to the ground against the water's bank. I lay motionless as he meandered around. After what seemed to be an eternity, he went back inside, and as soon as I thought it was safe, I eased into the water and began to swim in the channel.

As I reached the shallow water, I discovered something that I knew but had forgotten about – mud! With every step, my shoes bogged down in the mud, which made walking almost impossible. I wasn't sure I could travel like this. After each step, I had to exert a lot of effort just to free my feet from the mud. I soon had to admit that this was not going to work. So I eased back into the water and back to my cottage. I was so disappointed, and when I went back to bed, I broke down and sobbed like a baby. I was beginning to feel that all hope of returning to the ones I loved was gone. I felt that I was a prisoner for life!

After a small pity party, I regained my composer and rationalized that this was only a setback. There were other options that I could try. One was to take the pirogue and navigate to where Hagan left me. I could leave a note for Roscoe telling him where the boat was, and when the traders came, hopefully, they would take him there to retrieve it. The more I thought about that idea, the more I liked it. While that didn't remove the mud problem, I figured if I was near the boating channel, I could flag down a boater and catch a ride.

So, I got up again and wrote a note to Roscoe thanking him for saving my life and taking care of me, but I explained that I needed to return home. I told him where he could retrieve his pirogue, and then I attached the note to the door of his cottage. I quietly eased out into the water and headed toward my destination.

Although it was dark, I was able to get to the vicinity of my tree. When it was daylight, I easily found the cypress tree with the snag. After a short time and little effort, I found the tree with the fishing trap. I knew this was my tree! I got out onto the root mass and tied off the boat. From there, I waded until I felt I was a safe distance from being detected, and I climbed out of the water and up on top of another cypress root mass where I waited. I figured either I'd hear a motorboat in the canal with enough time to make it to the water or else Roscoe would come for his boat. Either way, I needed to stay hidden for the moment.

I waited and waited. Soon, the sun was up and it was getting hot. I got sleepy and eventually dozed off. I was awakened by the sound of a motorboat in the near distance. I quickly jumped into the water and tried to get to the channel in time to flag down the boater, but I only made it about halfway when he zipped by.

I knew from that episode that I needed to be closer to the channel, but I also needed to be far enough back in case Roscoe came for his boat. I glanced to check, and it was still tied to the tree. The thought had occurred to me that he might have slipped in while I was asleep, but he hadn't.

I made my way back into the swamp to better conceal myself from Roscoe. I realized I would have to stay hidden until he came for his boat, but after that, I should be able to get a little closer to the water channel. I climbed back into a tree close to where I was before. I watched all kinds of birds flying from tree to tree and envied their freedom. In the water, I could see several fish swim by near the surface. Most of them were bass, and once in a while, a nice-sized one eased by. When I was ready, I could probably shoot one with my bow and arrow.

Time dragged by and it was getting late into the day. I figured Roscoe would surely have come by now, but perhaps, this was not a day when the traders visited him. It was so late now that I knew it meant another night in the trees. I had been running on adrenaline all day, but now I realized I was very hungry, and the mosquitoes were beginning to bite me. I decided that I would go rob the fish trap of one catfish and have it for supper, although the thought of eating it raw was not very appealing to me for it was better than starving.

Just as I was about to slip down into the water, I heard a boat in the distance. I stopped and listened, and it seemed to be getting closer. Closer and closer it came until it was in view. It was Roscoe! I froze to the tree trunk just like a squirrel clinches to a limb. I only hoped that he didn't see me. I don't know what he would do to me if he did see me, and I didn't want to find out.

The traders dropped him off at his pirogue, and through the thick grove of cypress trees, I could see him standing up in it looking through the trees as if he was trying to find me. I didn't move a muscle in spite of the mosquito bites. Finally, he bade farewell to his trader friend who had given him a lift and pushed off with his push pole and eventually drifted out of sight.

I waited for another good ten minutes or so before easing over to the trap. I was surprised that he didn't check the trap and retrieve the fish, but he didn't. I grabbed a fish and then perched up on a tree about twenty feet from the channel. After choking down the fish, I dove down to the bottom of the water and grabbed a handful of mud and smeared it over my arms and face in hopes it might deter the mosquitoes. I think if may have helped, but it didn't stop them completely from feasting on me.

That night was really miserable. In addition to the mosquitoes, I kept hearing all kinds of animal sounds that I had never heard before. Occasionally, I would hear a large splash nearby and figured it was a gator attacking some prey. I hoped I wasn't in the sight of one of them. Although I was several feet above the water, I certainly didn't feel safe. Then there was the worry of snakes. Since I had no light, I could only see by the glow from the moon, which didn't give very much light.

Eventually, I detected the bright glow in the eastern horizon as the sun was about to make its appearance. I was so grateful to have survived another night. A gentle breeze began to blow after the sun was shining brightly, and this helped with the mosquito problem. I eased into the water and washed the mud off my body. As I was splashing around in the water, I heard a boat approaching from the north. I stashed my bow and arrows and quickly swam and waded to the edge by the open water of the channel. Once I could see the boat and could tell it was not one of Roscoe's friends, I swam out into the channel and started waving my hands frantically in hopes that the boater would see me.

Sure enough, he cut back on his motor as he passed by me, and then he circled around and eased back up to me. "Hey, Fella! Need some help?"

"I sure do. I need a lift to Hopes Landing. Can you help me?" "Maybe," he said as he extended his hand down to help pull me into his boat.

"What'ch doing out here in the middle of this swamp?" he asked. "It's a long story, but I have been lost out here for quite a while and trying to get back to Hopes Landing." "Hungry?" the good stranger asked.

"I sure am," I replied as he reached into his cooler and handed me a scrambled egg sandwich. I thanked him and told him that never had anything tasted so good to me.

I told him that I must look like a wild man since it had been a long time since I had been able to clean up. He smiled and said, "Hey, not a problem with me."

I sat in the middle seat of his boat and reminisced about the last time I traveled these waters with Sheriff Hagan and how there had been such a drastic change in my life since then.

After thirty minutes or so, the stranger said we were approaching Hopes Landing just around the bend and asked if there was a particular dock where I wanted to be dropped off. I told him the first one, and we soon eased up to the dock side. I shook his hand and told him that I would be more than happy to pay him for his kindness and help if I had any money, but the best I could do would be to drop him a check in the mail later. He insisted that would not be necessary, and after I thanked him again, he pushed off and was soon around the bend and out of sight.

Now, I was once again standing inside the city limits of Hopes Land and wondering what was ahead for me.

10
Chapter

As I stood there on the dock, I was thankful that I was out of the swamp. The sun was beaming down upon me with a gentle southern breeze that helped dry out my wet clothes. I sat on a nearby bench to gather my thoughts as to what I should do. The highest thing on my priority list was to call Dad. Depending on our conversation, I would then decide what to do after that.

Secondly, I needed to clean up some. Although I could not see myself, I knew I must be a sight to see. While I sat there, a sheriff deputy's car drove by, and my heart skipped a beat or two as I was very much afraid. I wondered why I came back here and not to somewhere else. Then I remembered my thinking was because I figured it was the closest place to where I was. I was somewhat familiar with the surroundings, and I assumed it was a safer place because Sheriff Hagan and his corrupt team had hopefully been removed from office. While all that seemed to make sense at the time, now that I was here, I was really nervous and cautious. In fact, I wasn't sure I wanted to leave the dock, but I knew I must.

It was only a block or two from the dock to the main street that runs through town. I was at the end near the convenience store. I thought I'd walk up there and check things out. I knew I looked like a bum and figured no one would recognize or want to help me. As I walked, I began to feel a little woozy and became very nauseated, but I kept walking. I made it to the street and waited for the traffic to clear before crossing, and all the time I was waiting, I expected to see a deputy sheriff's car drive past, but it didn't happen.

I soon crossed the street and walked into the store. I was trying to figure out how I was going to call Dad since I had no money, no identification, and certainly no credit card. I finally worked up enough courage to ask one of the customers if I could use his cell phone to make an important call, and he looked at me and said, "No way, Fella. Go back to the ghetto where you belong."

I thought that was a pretty rude remark, but I could understand why he had such an opinion of me. I guess the store manager must have seen what took place because almost immediately he approached me and asked me to leave his store before he called the cops. Calling the police was the last thing I wanted or needed, so I left without incident. As I was walking across the parking lot trying to figure out what to do, a man who I thought I recognized drove up to the gas pumps. I stopped in my tracks and stared for a few seconds, and then it hit me. It was Mike Hopkins, the athletic director for the high school who helped me find Logan's mother!

"Hey, Mr. Hopkins!" He looked up from pumping gas and saw me walking in his direction. As I got near enough for him to hear me without having to shout, I said, "Mr. Hopkins, I'm Richard Scroggins. Remember the LSU recruiter who wanted Allen to play football for us? May I have a minute with you?" By this time, I was really feeling sick and sweat had popped out on my forehead.

"Scroggins, what has happened to you?" he said.

"It's a long story, but I survived the grip of Hagan's swamp. I need to call my family to let them know I'm alive. May I use your cell phone?"

"Sure! By all means!" he replied as he motioned me to the passenger side of his car. I dialed Dad, but all I got was his voice mail. I left a message saying that I was alive and in Hopes Landing and that I needed a ride. I was feeling worse and told Mike that I was about to pass out. He quickly grabbed an ammonia strip from his athletic bag in the back seat that they used for ballplayers who get knocked out. He held it under my nose which revived me for a moment, but I told him that I was sick. He said he'd take me to his house and try to get some help for me.

I was really aching by the time we arrived at his house. He helped me out of the car and into the house. We were close to the same size, and he helped me get into a clean change of clothes. After changing, I lay down on some bedding that he had put on the couch. When he went to the kitchen, I heard his cell phone ring and him saying, "Hello, Mr. Scroggins. Richard is at my house but is pretty sick. I don't know what's wrong, but I really think we need to get him to the hospital, but I'm in no position to get him there." Then there was a pause as Mike was listening to Dad. After a few seconds and several "okays and yes sirs", Mike gave Dad his address.

I felt a real sigh of relief and then fell asleep.

When I woke up, I didn't know where I was but soon realized I was in a hospital some place. I had an IV in my arm with the monitor near my bed. I must have mumbled something because immediately Dad, Janet, and Talisa were standing by my bedside!

My first thought was that I must be dreaming, but all three in unison leaned over and hugged me. The emotions were high and the tears flowed freely as we were reunited once again. This seemed to be the most joyful few minutes of my life! As the hugs ended and they stood near my bedside, I couldn't believe my eyes.

"Seems like we've done this before," I jokingly said. "Where am I this time?"

Talisa kept holding my hand as Dad said I was in the Iberia Parish Hospital at Donaldsonville. My next question was how I got here and why. Dad said he could tell me the "how", but they needed me to fill in the blanks as to the "why".

I then began to tell the story of how Hagan sensed the FBI raid and took Taylor and me for a boat ride and that he shot Taylor and tossed him into the swamp, and I jumped out of the boat. They were all ears as I explained every detail of my episode in the swamp. They were very thankful that Roscoe had rescued me and taken care of me all those months, even though he didn't want me to leave the swamp. Talisa said she sure was glad I didn't stay and marry his daughter! I finished the story with me being sick and going to Mike Hopkins' house which was the last thing I remembered until now. They were absolutely astounded at the story I told.

As I had suspected, they all had assumed that I was dead. They said they even held a memorial service for me! I laughed at that and told them it would have been funny if I had walked in right in the middle of the service. I jokingly said that when I "really" die, they wouldn't have to fool with a service since I had already had one. Then I asked, "Did very many people come?" Janet swatted me on the arm.

Dad said, "The reason you are here is because you have what they call "*anisakis simplex.*" I had never heard of that before. The doctors were baffled for a while but finally narrowed it down to this." Naturally, I was concerned and wanted to know if it was treatable or not.

"You're going to be okay. Once they figured out what you had, they knew how to treat it, and in a few days, you should be as good as new. The mystery is how you contracted it in the first place."

"What do you mean?" I asked.

Dad went on to explain that the doctors said *anisakis simplex* is a rare parasitic roundworm that invades the gastrointestinal tract of humans. It comes from eating raw fish.

Immediately, when he mentioned raw fish, I thought about the catfish I ate the night before coming to Hopes Landing, which explained why I didn't start to feel bad until I got there.

Talisa jumped into the conversation and with a big smile said, "Richard, you look like a homeless person, but I love you just the same!" After she said that, I realized that I still had my long beard and shaggy long hair. Somewhere along the way, someone had cleaned me up and put me in a hospital gown, but they didn't shave my beard or cut my hair.

"What do you think about my beard?" Before she had time to answer, I said, "I think I'll keep it. It will be a reminder of just how important family and freedom really are."

By the time I had finished telling my story, Dad and Janet were sitting in the hospital room chairs, and Talisa was sitting on the bedside close to me and was holding my hand. Then I started with many of my questions. The first was how I got here to the hospital. Dad explained, "After receiving your phone call, I called Mike Hopkins because you had used his phone and his number showed up on my phone. He told me that you were sick and needed help.

I immediately called my FBI friends, and they arranged for an ambulance to pick you up and bring you here."

I picked up on Dad's reference to the FBI which led to my second question about Sheriff Hagan.

"Thanks to you and Taylor, we got enough video and evidence to put Hagan and his bunch away for a long, long time. Regretfully it ended for you two the way it did, but Hope's Landing is now under the authority of the state police until local officers can be elected and appointed. Son, thanks to you, Hope's Landing is a safe and good place to live. Not only were Hagen and his deputies exposed, but the investigation led to the mayor, city council, the school superintendent, and the school board who were all implicated and several arrests were made. In fact, several state officials are also being investigated. Richard, I wish you could have seen it. CNN got word of it and there were news people swarming around Hopes Landing like bees. Your picture was flashed on CNN as the one who set this sting in motion. While they were giving you recognition as a hero, they added the unfortunate disclaimer that you were missing and feared dead and that Hagen had not been captured.

"It was on national news that they thought I was dead?" I questioned.

"Yes, that's exactly right. Janet and I received telephone calls from all over the country from people extending their condolences." "This means everyone except you three and Coach Hopkins still thinks I'm dead?"

"Yeah, probably," Dad agreed.

"That means in all probability, I don't have a job and that my apartment has been rented to someone else. All my credit cards have probably been canceled, and on and on it goes."

"I hadn't thought about that, but you are probably right," Dad said.

"Wow!" I needed to come to grips with this reality. Knowing that we succeeded in getting rid of the corruption made me feel really good, but I wasn't sure I was ready to deal with the consequences brought about by the national media. I wondered if the people in Hopes Landing felt better, or if they had been under such a stronghold for so long that they didn't know any difference.

"Do they have any idea what happened to Sheriff Hagan?" I asked.

"Just that he got away. No one has been able to find a trace of him. Some think he may have killed himself by jumping into the swamp rather than face the consequences for what he had done. If he is ever found, he's history because of what his deputies confessed along with your surveillance information."

I told Dad that I overheard him and his chief deputy say they were heading for Mexico. He said he figured that might have happened.

Dad and Janet decided to go to the cafeteria for a bite of breakfast which left Talisa and me alone. When they left, Talisa leaned over to me, and I gave her the best hug that I could. While we were embracing each other, I whispered into her ear, "I was afraid I would never see you again, and I was worried that you already thought I was dead and had found someone else. Talisa, I never want you out of my life. As soon as I get up and around, will you marry me and be my wife forever?"

Without hesitation, she whispered back, "Oh Richard! You know that I will."

Nothing else was said for what seemed to be several minutes. We both enjoyed the moment of just holding one another.

Then, she broke the silence by saying, "I really like your beard. I hope you will keep it."

While she was sitting at the bedside, a nurse came in and said, "Well, Mr. Scroggins, it's good to see you are awake this morning. How are you feeling?"

I told her I was feeling great and was ready to go home.

She took all my vital signs and said the doctor would come by later, but from the way things looked, the infection was gone and that he would probably release me. That was good news also. This was turning out to be one of the best days of my life!

When Dad and Janet returned, we shared our engagement news with them. They were both very excited. Talisa had now been with them for almost six months and they had come to love her as a daughter, so this was good news to them. They said she had become a valuable asset to their company, and they didn't think they could run it without her.

As the nurse had thought, when the doctor came and checked me, he released me. He said since the infection was gone, there was no reason to keep me in the hospital and jokingly said they needed the bed for sick people. So within the hour, I was dressed in some clothes that Dad had brought me from home, and we left the hospital.

In cases where cars are abandoned, the state impounds them for up to six months before auctioning them off to some bargain shoppers. Dad said he had earlier checked and made arrangements for my car to be picked up and held at the local state trooper's impoundment center which wasn't far from the hospital so we drove there. After signing a few release papers, I had my car, my girl, and my life back. What a great day!

Dad and Janet headed back to Texas, but Talisa stayed with me. Dad left me some money, but until I got a copy of my driver's license, Talisa was to be my chauffeur. It had been almost six months since I disappeared, and there were many things I needed to check on, but first I wanted to go back to Hope's Landing. I wanted to visit with Logan's mother, and I wanted to visit the café where so much had happened to me. I also wanted to personally thank Mike Hopkins for helping me. This sounded good to Talisa, so once again, I was on the road to Hopes Landing.

This time as we drove into town, I didn't feel compelled to keep looking over my shoulder for a sheriff's car. We pulled into the café, and the original waiter that I first met took our orders. However, since my appearance had changed so much, she didn't recognize me. Soon our food was served, and Talisa talked non-stop while we were there. I told her the atmosphere here now was so different than it was before. I didn't see fear in the eyes of the people, and when a state trooper showed up, he was laughing and joking with all the people inside the cafe. I left feeling good that we had made a difference, and I was also glad that the waitress didn't recognize me. From there, we headed to Mike Hopkins' house. His car was not at home, but as I was writing him a note, he drove up. He recognized me from the other day and immediately invited us inside. I introduced Talisa to him, and he said his wife should be home soon.

Naturally, Mike wanted to know what happened, and I shared the details with him. He said, "What an amazing and incredible story! This should be made into a movie." I told him as I looked back on it, it really was an incredible story and that I was very fortunate to be alive.

Mike went on to tell us how much better things in town were now that the corruption was gone. The people were not afraid anymore to get out and go places. The school was under the school board of the neighboring parish until an election could be held to elect a new one. "Richard, the people of Hopes Landing can never repay you for what you have done for us and our community." I told him I was glad things were better and that I was just one of many who pulled off the sting operation.

From there, we headed to the home of Logan's mom. I still didn't have the consent papers that she needed to sign, but I felt much easier about visiting her. As we drove up, Talisa was amazed that people lived with so much water around them, and then when the dogs started going off, her amazement quickly changed to fear. We sat in the car until his mom walked out onto the front porch. I had to remember my appearance and that people didn't recognize me. I rolled the window down and called to tell her who I was. When she realized what I had said, she had a grin from ear to ear! She quickly rushed off the porch to my car and shooed the dogs away as she did. "Mr. Richard, we all thought you were…"

"Dead." I finished the sentence for her. "There are now two of us who survived the grip of Hagan's swamp. Allen and I should exchange stories of our survival." She invited us inside, and as usual, she offered us some cookies to eat. It had been a long time since I had homemade cookies, and they were delicious.

I asked her about Allen, and then I turned to tell Talisa that we knew him as Logan. His mom said that after all the arrests and stuff took place, Allen came to see her and told her that he was planning to go to college. A man was with him who had some papers she needed to sign. She said they talked for a while before they left, and the man said that was all she needed to do. She was happy to tell us that since then, Allen had been home two more times.

"Mr. Scroggins, I owe so much to you and your courage. I will never be able to repay you for what you have done and for your determination that brought my son home. Under very harsh circumstances, you never gave up." I assured her that I was the one who was blessed, and I was so glad to hear that she and Allen had gotten together. After a nice visit, Talisa and I left.

Talisa, in her charming manner said, "Where to, Sir?" I told her, "To Baton Rouge." In a couple of hours, we drove up to my apartment, and I knocked on the door. As I feared, someone else answered the door and I simply excused myself and asked where the office was. Of course, I knew but I needed something to say.

We went to the office, and when I told the office manager who I was, she was very apologetic for renting out my apartment. I told her that I understood and figured if the roles had been reversed, I would have done the same thing. She did say that all my belongings were in a storage building awaiting auction. In cases like mine, they were required to hold the personal property for six months to allow the next-of-kin an opportunity to make any claims. She anticipated my next question as she was turning through her day planner and said, "The auction is scheduled for Saturday, three weeks from now.

I asked her how I could get my stuff before it was auctioned off and she gave me the address and phone number of the storage facility and said probably all I needed to do was to pay the rent and they would let me have it. I thanked her and we left.

It was getting late, but I wanted to make one more stop. I wanted to go see Coach Bevels. Soon, Talisa and I were in front of his office door, and I tapped on it before walking in. As we entered, he looked up from his desk and said, "May I help you?"

11

Chapter

Icould tell by Coach Bevels' face that he had no idea who we were. "Hello, Coach, I'm Richard Scroggins." You should have seen his face. He looked as though he had seen a ghost! "Richard! I thought ..."

I interrupted him and said, "I know. Everybody else did too, and I should have been. But with the Good Lord looking over me, here I am after living six months in the swamps."

"Man, I can't tell you what a thrill it is for me to see you! You will never know what we all went through trying to adjust to your not being here. Logan took it worse than all the rest of us because he felt it was his fault that you died – or supposedly died. Tell me what happened."

I sat down on the edge of his desk and told him my story. I left nothing out and told him I had only learned earlier today that the corruption in Hopes Landing had been disrupted and that Logan had been able to go visit his mother.

"Yeah. He and I went down there several weeks ago and I wish you could have seen their reunion. Normally, I'm not an emotional type of guy, but I couldn't stop the tears from running down my cheeks as I stood by and watched them. Richard, all this happened because of you. You are certainly one of a kind."

"Aw, Coach. You're making me out to be more than I am. I just wanted Logan to come here and play football. How's he doing?"

"Oh, he's doing great. He fits in well with all the other players and is trying really hard to do what the coaches want him to do. It seems as if when he thought you had died, he felt that he had something to prove. So, he started working harder than all the others in the weight room, as well as out on the track running, to get in shape. Richard, he's the real deal."

"I knew that he was. Can I see him?"

"Sure. He should be in the dorm at this time of day. I'll give him a call."

I had already introduced Talisa and Coach Bevels, and while we waited for Logan to show up, I told him that we were planning to be married soon. He was really excited to hear that bit of news, but then a long somber look came on his face. I knew something was wrong, so I asked him what the matter was.

He said it was exciting that we were getting married, but then he added, "Richard, I hate to tell you that when we thought you weren't coming back, we filled your position as a recruiter. You no longer have a job with LSU."

"Hey Coach, don't feel bad about that because I assumed that would have happened. Is there anything else I can do? Can you make a spot for me somewhere else?"

"I don't know. Let me probe around and see what I can come up with, but no promises."

I told him I understood as Logan was walking into the office. Like everyone else, he didn't recognize me, but he looked long and hard at Talisa as if he had seen her before but couldn't put a name with the face.

Coach Bevels said, "Logan, I want to introduce you to someone very special. I'd like you to meet Mr. Richard Scroggins." Logan whirled around with his jaw dropped. By this time, I had my arms wide open, and he immediately rushed to me and embraced me and squeezed me so hard that I actually had a hard time breathing.

While we were embraced, he said, "Mr. Scroggins, thank you!

Thank you! Thank you!"

Finally, he pulled away, and I said, "Now there are two of us who have survived Hagan's swamp."

He gave me a thumbs up and said, "Mr. Scroggins, I'm going to make you proud of me; you just wait and see!"

"Logan, you already have, and I can hardly wait to see what you will become."

The conversation lasted for a few more minutes before I told Coach Bevels and Logan that we needed to leave as we were driving to East Texas tonight. And then, I explained the deal about my apartment and that I had no place to stay plus Talisa needed to get back to work.

She looked surprised that we were going to Texas tonight, but seemed pleased to do so. I knew it was a six or seven-hour drive which should put us there around midnight. I told Coach Bevels and Logan that I'd keep in touch, and then we left.

The drive home was good. The traffic was light, and the conversation was delightful. We jumped from football to careers to music to church to weddings. The more I was around Talisa, the more I knew I loved her. The time passed quickly, and before we realized it, we were driving into Dad's yard.

We tried to be quiet so as not to wake Janet and Dad, but as soon as we opened the door, the hall light came on. Janet had just gone to bed and was not yet asleep, so she got up. The three of us had a cup of hot chocolate while I told Janet about our visit with Coach Bevels and Logan.

The next morning, we all had breakfast together, and the three of them got ready for work at the Private Investigator's office. It seemed strange that I was unemployed. After everyone had left, I wondered what I would do with myself all day. I had worked since I was a teenager, and except for weekends, I was never at home during the day. I took a cup of coffee and walked around the farm and reminisced about old times. I had so many happy memories of this farm, and I never got tired of the beauty of east Texas, and especially the beautiful sunrises and sunsets. As I was strolling and enjoying the beauty, I had a deep gnawing in the pit of my stomach that Sheriff Hagan was probably free and enjoying his life somewhere. I felt that shouldn't be happening since he had caused so much heartache to so many for so long. I wanted more than anything to see him brought to justice! The thought kept running through my head that since I was unemployed, I had the time to go look for him and that was what I needed to do. The problem with that idea was that I had no legal authority to do anything, and secondly, I had no idea how or where to find him.

About mid-morning, the idleness and thoughts of Hagan got the best of me. I went to the office to discuss my feelings with Dad. I always had a very warm feeling when I entered that office. I felt especially warm today when Talisa was the first person I saw, and I couldn't help but notice how beautiful she looked. She immediately came over and gave me a short, dignified kiss. I asked her if it was convenient for me to talk to Dad, and she poked her head into his office to see and then motioned for me to go into his office.

"Hey, Richard! Are you getting bored?" Dad asked.

"I guess I am a little, but there is something I want to discuss with you." Then I told him how it was bothering me that I assumed Hagan was footloose and fancy-free, and that I had an urgent need to see him brought to justice. I told him it was like people needing to have a graveside service for a loved one in order to bring closure to their death. I told him that I had no idea what to do or how to do it and asked if he had any suggestions.

He told me that it was not my job to do anything and that I should leave it up to the authorities to take care of Robert Hagan. I told him I understood that, but since I didn't have a job, I had time on my hands and it would be easy for me to go look for him.

Dad reminded me that I was thinking with my emotions and not rationally. He suggested that I do what he taught me to do as a child, which was to sit down and write on paper the pros and cons of what I was thinking, and he felt that common logic would tell me to forget it. Deep down I knew that he was right, but I couldn't shake the overwhelming feeling that I needed to be doing something.

I asked him if I did go looking for him, what could I do if I found him? He said the only legal thing I could do would be to notify the proper authorities telling them where he was and then let them handle it. I told him I wouldn't trust the local law officials wherever he might be in case he "had them under his thumb" as he did in Hopes Landing, so he said that perhaps, the FBI, the CIA, or Homeland Security should be notified. That sounded good to me.

"Dad, could I work for your agency and be one of your investigators?" He said he would have to give that some thought, but he didn't have a license or authority to do private investigating in a foreign country and reminded me that I thought Hagan might be in Mexico.

"Just a thought," I said as I stood up to leave. "Richard, the best thing for you to do is to drop it." "Yes, sir. I guess you are right."

I invited Talisa to join me for lunch. We went it JJ's Hamburger Shop down the street from their office. I told her about my conversation with Dad and what his advice was, and she agreed with him totally. After lunch, I returned home and sat on the front porch stewing about what I should do. I knew logically what would be best, but I couldn't shake it emotionally. Perhaps if I had a job to occupy my mind, I wouldn't feel such a desire to see Hagan behind bars where he belonged.

I called Coach Bevels to see if he had any information about anyone needing a recruiter, or if there might be something else I could do at LSU. As I expected, he didn't have any leads but promised to keep his ears open and to let me know if anything turned up. I looked at the job want-ads in the newspaper and on the computer, but nothing I was interested in jumped out at me. There were some ads for a convenience store cashier, a librarian clerk, and a dock man needed at the feed store. Maybe I could do some undercover work for Dad!

I went back to his office and asked if he had a leg-work job for me to do temporarily at the detective agency. He said there was an insurance injury claim that the insurance company felt was fraudulent, and they had hired his agency just today to take pictures to support their suspicions. I was excited and more than willing to do that! The man was also named Richard, and he lived in Tyler.

Dad gave me the information on where he lived and how he claimed to have a wrenched back that kept him mostly in bed and that he was expecting a large settlement from the insurance company. He also gave me the equipment that I needed, including a watch and ring to take pictures and send messages like what I had used in Hopes Landing. My adrenaline soon started pumping, and I was eager to get started gathering evidence without being detected. The next morning, I was staked out down the street from Richard's house in Tyler. What I hadn't thought about was having so much time alone during the stakeout, which led to me thinking again about trying to find Hagan. After a few hours of waiting and watching, Richard walked out of his house. As he was headed toward his car, he reached down and picked up a limb that had fallen from a tree and flung it over a fence. I thought he wouldn't have been able to do that if his back was so bad. He got into his car and drove away, and just like on a television show, I trailed at a safe distance behind him. I followed him to Lowes Hardware Store.

We both went inside, and I kept a close watch on him. There appeared to be nothing wrong with his back as he seemed to have no problem picking up several gallons of paint. I used the ring camera and got some close-up shots of him lifting the paint from the shelf into his basket and then from the basket onto the check-out counter. I followed him back to his house where he disappeared behind his garage door. I thought it would be good if I had some evidence of him painting. He lived on *Red Bird Lane*. I keyed in *Red Bud Lane* on my GPS and it defaulted to *Red Bird Lane*.

After giving him time to get started with the painting, I wore the ring camera and watch recorder and rang his doorbell. He came to the door with the paintbrush in his hand, and I excused myself and told him that my GPS led me to this address instead of *Red Bud Lane* and I wondered if perhaps, they were the same road. He said they weren't, and I apologized for the mistake and asked him if he knew where *Red Bud Lane* was. Of course, he didn't, and then I said, "Looks like you are doing some painting."

"Yeah, my wife has been on me for several weeks to paint our bedroom and bath, so I finally gave in and decided to get it done."

"I don't envy you," I said. "I don't like to paint, and it seems that every time I do, my back is out of whack for days."

"Well, I don't mind it once I get everything taped off and ready, which is the part I don't like. But it's never bothered my back," he replied.

I then excused myself and left. I had several good shots of him holding the paintbrush along with his recorded statement. The rest of the day was boring, so about mid-afternoon, I headed back home. Over the next few days, I continued to collect evidence on Richard's supposedly back problem, and perhaps the most important were pictures of him on the golf course swinging the golf clubs with no sign of any back problem. Finally, Dad said I had enough evidence and asked me to put together a package to present to the claims department of the insurance company. I felt a bit nervous making the presentation, but they all seemed to appreciate the information and complimented me on a job well done. But now, more than ever, I still had the urge to seek out Robert Hagan.

After a few more jobs with Dad and the passing of several months, I finally told him that I couldn't rest until I looked for Hagan. He didn't seem too surprised as he sensed that I still had that burning inside of me. I asked him how and where I should start.

He said, "Son, if you are dead set on doing this, you first need to understand that it is an expensive venture not to mention a dangerous one. It's dangerous enough here in our country, but when you go to one of the Central or South American Countries, the risk increases - if for no other reason than your skin color leads to suspicions. Once you understand those dangers, I'd start by asking the FBI for assistance. If you work through my office as a private investigator, perhaps they can use you as a volunteer undercover agent. That means you would have access to their intelligence as well as their technology. Without their help, you would, without a doubt, be committing suicide. "

"Can you set up a meeting for me with the FBI?" I asked. "Son, are you sure?"

"Yes Sir, I'm sure. Dad, this is something I simply have to do."

Seeing how serious I was, he said he'd make a few phone calls tomorrow.

That night, I told Talisa about my decision. As expected, she was very distraught about it but said quite frankly, "I'm going with you!" I wasn't expecting that and tried to talk her out of it, but she insisted and argued that since she could speak the language in Mexico, she would be a big help. She also pointed out that a couple would not be as suspicious as a single man nosing around, and I had to admit that she had some valid points. I told her that I'd think about it during the night.

That night a million things ran through my head, so I got very little sleep. Some of those thoughts centered on Talisa going with me. Since she insisted on going, I decided that I'd let her but I wanted us to get married first and go as husband and wife on a honeymoon trip.

The next morning, when I mentioned the marriage idea to her, she got all excited and enthusiastically agreed. We shared our plans with Dad and Janet, and they were cautiously concerned and encouraged us to seriously consider what we were about to do.

All I could think about for the rest of the day was getting married and putting the love of my life in harm's way. But on the other hand, going was her idea and she'd have it no other way. After Talisa got off work, I picked her up and we went to the edge of the creek and sat and talked about us and this venture I was considering. We discussed all the pros and cons that we could think of, and we finally decided to proceed as first planned. We both recognized the risks and were willing to accept them. Before we left, we decided to get married as soon as possible. We agreed to get a marriage license tomorrow and then have the justice of the peace marry us after the three-day wait requirement.

We enjoyed sitting by the creek and watching the ripples as they flowed past us. Talisa had been living with Dad and Janet for several months, but she hadn't ventured out much on her own and seemed to be enjoying nature as much as I did. We enjoyed watching the squirrels scurrying around from tree to tree, looking at the wildflowers, watching the beautiful sunset, and we both hated to leave the peaceful surroundings.

When we got home and told Dad and Janet of our decision, they were apprehensive but supportive. Dad told me that he talked with someone at the FBI agency in Dallas and that they agreed to send an agent down later in the week to talk with me. I couldn't believe so much was happening all at once. It was really overwhelming.

The next day, Talisa and I went to the courthouse as planned and got our marriage license at the county clerk's office. A few days later, I was in the office when a man came in and asked to speak to Dad. I showed him the correct office, and when he walked in, I heard Dad say, "Albert! Albert Jennings! Why I haven't seen you in a month of Sundays! How are you doing?"

The man extended a similar greeting as they faced each other and shook hands. Then Dad motioned for me to come into his office and introduced me to his long-time friend. They were friends years ago while working for the Houston Police Department, and now Albert was working for the FBI.

After a little bit of catching up on each other's personal lives, the conversation made its way to me and the real reason Albert was there. He asked me if I definitely wanted to look for Robert Hagan, and I assured him that I did. Then he asked if I knew where he was, and I told him that I overheard him say that he was heading for Mexico, but that was almost a year ago. So no, I didn't know where he was. He grinned when he said, "Well, it is probably hard to find someone when you don't know where to look for them!"

Agent Jennings said the FBI didn't know where he was either. He said, "While Hagan was a bad guy, and now a fugitive, our department is spending the majority of the time and resources monitoring what they believe to be terrorist cells. Ever since the bombing in New York on 9/11, the agency has rearranged its list of priorities, and people like Hagan, unless they are a threat to the security of our country, get pushed to the bottom of the list. So, no one has been assigned to track him down. Even though he shot and killed one of our agents, it is sad to say that still does not move him up very far on our "most wanted" list. So, Richard, any information you have is likely more than we have."

I told Agent Jennings that I was disappointed to hear what I was hearing because I was expecting a lot of help and information from the FBI. He said, "This is not to say we won't help, because we want him too. We are willing to provide technology, transportation, and manpower short term, like on a raid, but what I am saying is that we don't have any logistic information as to where Hagan is. I will tell you that the last hint we had was that he was no longer in Mexico, but somewhere in Idaho."

I guess I had a look of doubt on my face as he added, "The reason I say "hint" is that one of our surveillance teams who monitor cameras at airports saw a man who looked like Hagan boarding a plane from Mexico City going to Hailey, Idaho. That was almost six months ago, and we haven't seen a trace of him nor heard anything about him since then. We know he, or whoever looked like him, arrived in Idaho because we have pictures of him leaving the plane, but after that, we can't say. He may have headed up to Canada, or he may be hiding out in the city. Perhaps, he has barricaded himself up in the mountains someplace. We just don't know. He may have left the area completely, but we don't think he left on a commercial flight. However, with his contacts, he may have had someone fly in with a small plane and smuggle him somewhere else, or he could have purchased a car and driven himself to almost any place."

I was astonished and bewildered. "What should I do?" I asked. Dad asked Agent Jennings if they had any cell phone chatter from him, and he said, "We did early on while he was in Mexico, but nothing in a good while." Then he looked at me and said, "I appreciate your willingness to look for him, and I'm sorry I don't have any solid information."

I told him that while I was disappointed, I certainly understood, but I also wondered if there was a possibility of gathering some information.

He replied that there was always a possibility. "We have agents always monitoring and listening to activity. As I said earlier, the interest now is primarily looking for terrorist activity, but as long as we have our ears and eyes open, Hagan might cross into our radar. But gathering recognizance just on Hagan is unlikely."

"What should I do?" I asked again.

Agent Jennings said, "This is what I suggest."

12

Chapter

I was all ears as to what Albert Jennings had to say. He said if I was serious about tracking down Robert Hagan (which I was) then I should let the FBI sponsor my activities. If Dad would employ me as a private investigator, then the Bureau could use me as a volunteer agent which meant they would cover my expenses while serving in that capacity as well as furnish me with whatever equipment I might need.

Then he said, "If I were you, I'd start by interrogating some of the people who were arrested in Hopes Landing to see if they might have a clue as to Hagan's whereabouts. If you get a lead, then we would be willing to assist you in following that lead, but we don't have the manpower to back you. If you find Hagan, notify us, and we will move in and make the arrest since you would have no legal authority to do so. Does this sound like something you want to tackle?"

"Absolutely!" I eagerly replied.

"It will take a few days for me to get you into the system, but as soon as I have things set up, I'll notify you. Now, Richard, you understand that while we will fund your expenses, as a volunteer you will receive no salary or personal compensation."

"Yes, sir," I answered. "But I really don't need anything more than you picking up the tab. Just one more thing," I said.

"What's that?"

"I had planned on taking my wife with me which we thought might help remove suspicions; any problem with that?"

He thought for a moment and then said, "No problem."

After that, Agent Jennings and Dad said their farewells as they walked out to the street. I sat in Dad's office rather stunned at what was about to happen. I could hardly wait to tell Talisa!

When Dad got back in his office, I asked what he thought about everything. He said he felt better about me pursuing Hagan under the umbrella of the FBI. He also said he felt better with me pursuing in Idaho than in Mexico. "Interior Mexico is a very dangerous place for a Gringo," he added.

Then I asked him if it would be alright for me to take Talisa out of the office for the rest of the afternoon as I wanted to fill her in on what was happening. As I expected, he said it would be fine and then said, "We need to start learning how to get along without her as it seems she will soon be gone with you for a while."

I smiled and said, "That's right."

I took Talisa back to JJ's as she really liked the french-fries there. While we were eating, I told her all that had happened, and she listened very intently to every word. Once she realized that we would probably not be going to Mexico, she was concerned that I would not need her to go with me. I explained to her that we were now a team, and wherever I went, I planned on her being with me.

Soon, the conversation changed to our wedding. We agreed to go to the Justice of the Peace on Monday and have him marry us without any fan-fair. Most likely, our honeymoon would be in Boise, Idaho.

For most of the weekend, I was on the computer studying maps and landmarks of Idaho. I knew very little about that part of our country and had never been any closer than a trip once to Santa Fe, New Mexico, trying to recruit a football player for LSU. I knew very little about mountain survival. I learned that two major mountainous areas were divided by the Salmon River. One area was called the Salmon Mountains and the other was called the Bitterroot Mountains. If Robert Hagan was isolated in either of those two regions, then we might never find him.

I decided not to shave or cut my hair in order to have a different appearance than I had the last time Hagan saw me. When I came out of the swamp, people I knew well didn't recognize me, so maybe he wouldn't either. But then no one was certain that he was the man who boarded the plane in Mexico. The man on the camera looked like Hagen, but they had no proof it was him. Oh well, Idaho would be a nice place for a honeymoon anyway.

Monday was a very eventful day in my life. Talisa and I went to the JP's office to be married. No one went with us, so the office secretary stood beside Talisa and the building janitor stood by me. The ceremony was short and sweet, and the important thing was that the judge signed the marriage license and had it recorded by the county clerk. We were now Mr. and Mrs. Richard Scroggins!

The next major event that happened was that Albert Jennings came by the office and told us that everything was set up and that I was good to go. He gave me an identification badge and number to use in communicating with the FBI agents or agency. My code name was *Goat Man,* and he gave me an identification number to use as well as a telephone number I could use in order to give or receive information.

That night, Talisa and I stayed with Dad and Janet and made plans to go to the Louisiana State Jail tomorrow to interrogate the deputies who were a part of the Hopes Landing corruption. Dad and Janet were aware that this was our wedding night and made a special effort to give us our privacy which we both appreciated. It was wonderful that we each now had a partner for life.

The next morning, I was excited and eager to get on the road. I really didn't know what to expect, but when we got to the state jail, I showed the security guard my identification badge, and he made a telephone call before he escorted me to a visitation room. Talisa had to wait in the lobby.

The first guy who was brought to me was the deputy that I first met in the café at Hopes Landing and who had given me such a hard time. When we made eye contact, he recognized me and said, "Well, I'll be! You must be Lazarus from the dead." I was very surprised that he recognized me since no one else had seemed to do so.

"That's pretty close," I said. "But I'm really looking for the big man, Hagan. I know he is in Idaho and thought you might be willing to help me some."

"What's in it for me?" he asked.

"Can't say for sure. You know how the system works. The help you give us may determine the amount of time you serve. A lot of help might get you down to just a few years."

"You don't really think I would snitch on my friend, do ya?"

"No, not really, but it seems to me that your "so-called friend" left you behind to take the rap while he is enjoying the fresh mountain air. Oh well, I thought it was worth a shot." Then I got up and headed to the door to ask the guard to take him back to his cell.

Before I got there, he cried out, "Wait! I might have some information!"

I looked back and said to him, "Too late. You had your chance. I'll get what I want from some others who were involved in your racket." Then the guard took the deputy back to his cell. All the while he kept saying, "Wait! I'll tell you what you want to know! Just give me another chance!"

I figured I'd let him stew about it for a while as I was talking to some of the others. I then visited with three other inmates, including the city mayor. Only the mayor seemed to have any useful information, but he was also reluctant to talk until I told him that the deputy had agreed to a deal and that I knew about the hideout in Idaho. I was bluffing, but it seemed to hit a nerve with him.

I told him the only thing I didn't know was which mountain range Hagen was in, but with a little effort, I could find him with or without his help. He thought about that for a few minutes and then said he didn't know for sure, but there used to be a ski resort in the Bitterroot Mountains near Sun Valley that closed down a few years ago because their lifts didn't meet state safety codes.

"The cartel in Mexico bought the lodge for a refuge. I'm not sure he is there, but that's where I would start."

I kept up my bluff and said, "At least your story agrees with the deputy's. I will see that your cooperation is noted to the parole board." Then I left.

On the way back home, Talisa and I were both excited and ready to go to Idaho. I used my cell phone to call the 800 number that I was given and was dispatched to Agent Jennings. I told him what I had found out, and he seemed pleased. I asked if I needed to fly to Idaho or drive. He said I definitely needed to fly and that he'd arrange for me to have a four-wheel-drive vehicle when I arrived. He said if I drove, my Texas plates would cause us to stand out like a sore thumb. He told me to wait at home until I received two airline tickets as well as a credit card from the agency. Then he closed by saying, "After you get your tickets and card, catch the next plane out and good luck."

A few hours later, we were back home in East Texas, and naturally, Dad and Janet wanted to know every detail about how our day had gone. They were pleased with my report. I told them that I would be receiving some tickets and a credit card at their office, and I would like for them to be on the watch for them and let me know when they arrived. They agreed to do so.

That night, I got back on the computer and printed off maps around Sun Valley. I was able to get both topographical and geographical maps as well as satellite photos of the area. I printed a lot of information and pictures and compiled them in a notebook for later reference. One thing I learned, despite the beautiful mountain villages nestled around several rivers, it was also very rugged terrain once you left the main roads. Sun Valley was one of three villages within a few miles of each other. Hailey was the largest of the three and had a commercial airport that accommodated both Sky West and Delta Airlines. After doing some research, I figured we would fly into Friedman Memorial Airport in Hailey.

I told Talisa that I had a cousin named Sonny who went to the Grand Canyon area a few years ago to try to locate someone who may have been held captive there. I told her that after fail-ing to find the man he was looking for, he ended up going on a ship to Yemen, and she was eager to hear the entire story which I shared with her. She was amazed at all he did. I told her I hoped we didn't have to go beyond Idaho to conclude our search.

Together, we viewed the regions around Sun Valley trying to get an idea of where Hagan might be. He could easily be in Hailey, Ketchum, or Sun Valley as they were all in close proxim-ity and each catered to winter tourists which meant there were many daily and weekly room accommodations, as well as long-term lease agreements, where he could be staying. I felt that even though we may have the region nailed down, it would still be like trying to find a needle in a haystack. Before we went to bed that night, we both felt that we knew the area quite well from study-ing the photo images that were posted on Google.

The next day, a package addressed to me was delivered to Dad's office. I opened it to find our tickets to Friedman Memorial Airport plus two credit cards - one in my name and the other in Talisa's. There was also a note telling us the name of the car rental agency where we were to go to pick up our SUV. It also said we had room reservations in the Hailey Hotel. In addition, there was a note saying a woman named *Betsy* worked at the Hailey Hotel and that we should contact her. I was to tell her I was known as *Goat Man* and that she would have additional instructions for me. I was amazed at how quickly and thoroughly the FBI Agency had acted.

I rushed around taking care of last-minute details, and the next morning Janet drove us to the airport in Tyler where we boarded an American Airline commuter flight to Dallas - Ft. Worth Airport. Soon we were on our way to Boise, Idaho. From there, we would go to Hailey. The flights were pleasant, and the weather conditions were unusually calm for November. We made connections without any trouble, and a Jeep Cherokee was waiting for us just as Albert Jennings had said. We registered at the Hailey Hotel, and I looked at the name tags of the clerks, but I didn't see Betsy on any of them. I asked a girl if Betsy was working today, and she said she was working as the cashier in the restaurant. I thanked her as she gave us the keys to our room which was on the sixth floor.

Before we got on the elevator, I peeked in the restaurant and saw Betsy. She was a beautiful young lady who looked to be about twenty-five. I wondered if she was the "right" Betsy as I had imagined her to be a much older woman. After waiting a few minutes, we went into the restaurant and waited until there were no customers at the register. I introduced Talisa and myself to her and said, "Sometimes my friends call me *Goat Man.*"

"Really? That is a rather unusual name. To what room would you like your meal delivered?" I told her room 608, and then we walked to the elevator without looking back at her.

About 9:30, there was a knock on the door followed by someone saying, "room service." I opened the door only to find Betsy outside. I quickly invited her in, and she was much more friendly and personable than she had been in the restaurant. She sat down on the bed and seemed to feel comfortable around us. She said she had been expecting us but was looking for someone older than us. I replied with the same sentiment, and we all got a laugh about the whole matter.

Then she got to the point. She said she had been placed out here almost a year ago to be a watchdog for terrorists. The FBI had information that led them to believe someone was making plans to attack a popular public resort, and this part of Idaho has some of the best resorts in the country. She said she was also a contact person for the agency. "I understand you are looking for a man named Robert Hagan - is that right?"

I told her she was correct as I showed her his picture from a year ago. She said she didn't remember seeing anyone who looked like him, but that he could certainly be in the area and not stay at this hotel. I asked her if she knew of an abandoned ski slope around Sun Valley, and she said there were at least a dozen of them, and probably more. "If they fail some type of safety inspection, it usually costs more to bring them up to standards than it does to build a new one. So there are many in the surrounding mountains that have been bought by the private sector to be used for sporting clubs, wealthy individuals, businesses, and such. They use the facilities for social and political gatherings."

"How can we get to them?" I asked.

"You can drive to some of them, but some have been abandoned a long time and the roads have not been maintained, so you need to either walk in or ride on horseback," she said with a cute smile. "Also, some are enclosed behind a gate that requires a code to enter as the owners don't want anyone coming in who hasn't been invited. It would not be surprising to me if the man you are looking for would have been invited to stay at any of those." Then she added that if we needed anything, we should discretely let her know and she'd do what she could to accommodate us. I thanked her for her help, and as she was leaving, she laid a map on the bed that showed where all the abandoned lodges were located. I was amazed that she knew where I wanted to go before we had even talked about it. Then I wondered what else she knew about me. I figured time would tell. After she left, both Talisa and I were amazed that she was a federal agent. Talisa said, "No one would ever expect her as such because of her cuteness," and I agreed.

We were both tired and decided to call it a day. I woke up early the next morning and made coffee in the courtesy coffee pot. I tried to be as quiet as possible so I wouldn't wake Talisa. With my cup of coffee, I sat at the table in the corner of the room and studied the maps and photos of the area as well as the maps that Betsy had left. I laid out an orderly plan to visit the abandoned ski lodges. I thought we should begin with the open lodges nearest Sun Valley in hopes of locating the old, abandoned ones and then work our way down from there toward Hailey.

After a few minutes, Talisa woke up and said the smell of the freshly brewed coffee made her want to get out of bed. She looked so beautiful with her messed-up hair and flannel nightshirt. I was so very happy that we had gotten married as she brightened my days so much. We both sat on the bed and drank our coffee while discussing the plans I had for the day. Before long, we were dressed and eating breakfast in the hotel restaurant, but apparently, Becky wasn't working. Perhaps, she would come in later today since she apparently worked the evening shift. But even if she had been working, she probably would have acted as if she didn't know who we were.

After breakfast, we made a twenty-minute drive from Hailey to Sun Valley. The scenery was nothing short of breathtaking. The fresh snow was so beautiful. We traveled along Sun Valley Road which followed Timber Creek. I told Talisa that this was the second most beautiful place I had ever seen and that it was close to number one, which was east Texas. As we approached the resort skiing area, I told Talisa that there were two mountains that had active ski slopes and they were Bald Mountain and Dollar Mountain. From Betsy's maps, it looked as if there were some abandoned resorts on the range behind Bald Mountain, so I thought that was where we needed to start our search.

We drove into the parking lot at the ski lodge and walked into the restaurant at the base of the slopes. This was where people bought their lift tickets, and so it was here we began our inquest.

13

Chapter

Talisa and I talked about the best way to approach our search. Should we flash Hagan's picture around in hopes that someone might recognize him? Perhaps he has been around here for several months and is well known. The risk in doing that is if someone who knows him saw the picture and alerted him, he would likely break and run. Also, he may have the entire town under his control as he did in Hopes Landing.

Another option was just to snoop around and see what turns up. After discussing what we thought was best, we agreed that I would pretend to be a writer who was up here doing a story on ski resorts, particularly old ones that were no longer being used. Hopefully, that would give us reason to be asking questions and taking pictures.

Before we left the car, I put on my camera ring and Talisa wore the recording watch. We decided that we made a good team. We each took a deep breath and then opened the car doors and briskly marched into the ski lodge. Once inside, we stood around for a few minutes taking inventory of where things were located, and then we made our way over to the ski lift ticket counter. A young man who looked to be in his early twenties was behind the counter. He could have easily been a college student working his way through school.

We walked up, and he professionally said, "Good morning. How can I help you?" I told him my name was Richard and that I was writing a story about abandoned ski lodges. "Are there any nearby that have been closed within the past ten years?"

As I expected, he had no idea so I asked him if there was someone I could speak with who might know. He excused himself and went into a nearby office that appeared to have a double pane glass. After a brief absence, he soon returned with an older man. He introduced himself as Lawson Davis. I told Mr. Davis who we were and what I wanted, and he said, "Mr. Scroggins, this is an unusual request, but I think I might be able to help you. Will you please come into my office? As we went into the room, I noticed the title *Lodge Manager* beside Davis' name.

I showed him the map that Betsy had given to me, and I ad-libbed by saying, "There is a marketing firm that has an interest in what happens to old, outdated ski lodges. I'm supposed to research and report to them my findings after which they will decide if making such purchases would be a lucrative business venture. Can you shed any light on the matter for me?"

As he studied the map, he said there were five lodges on Bald Mountain or Dollar Mountain. He pointed to the nearest one called *Timber Creek Lodge.* He said that it closed about three years ago and was bought by Prudential Insurance Company. They have their winter conferences there, and even though it is a risk, they operate the lift, which is now considered to be a private resort for their employees. This means that they are not inspected or regulated by the state's safety requirements.

The second lodge here on your map used to be called *White Cap Lodge.* It was purchased by the San Diego Padres. Like the first, it is a business investment but I'm not really sure how they are using it.

The third resort is called *Black Bear Lodge.* It has been closed for almost ten years. It is in the outback part of the Bitter Root mountain range. I can't tell you very much about it. It was initially bought by some rich oilman from the Middle East, but a few years ago it was rumored that he sold it to some people from Mexico.

While no one knows for sure, it is thought to belong to a drug cartel, but as long as they leave us alone, we leave them alone."

I interrupted him with a question, "How do I get to the places and interview some of the staff?"

"Well, the first two are easy. You just drive up to them like you got here today. But the third one can only be reached by foot or by air. It appears that most traffic in and out of there is by helicopter. What used to be a road was wiped out a few years ago by a mudslide during the wettest spring in Idaho history. Some hold to the idea that the mudslide had a little human help, but that was never proven. And if you go there, I would not expect them to be too friendly toward you and your story."

"Thanks for the advice. It sounds like we ought to skip that one. What about the other two on Dollar Mountain?" I felt I had the information that I was after, but needed to play the role to completion, so I appeared interested in what he said about them.

After he finished, I thanked him for his time and told him that he had been most helpful. And then we left. As we were walking to the jeep, I asked Talisa if she knew where we should go, and she saluted as she said, "Yes sir, Sherlock!" We decided to go back to the hotel and talk with Betsy. On the way, we took time out to visit some of the quaint little shops in the downtown area of Ketchum. While we didn't buy very much, we did enjoy some ice cream from a local creamery.

After killing a couple of hours, we figured Betsy should now be at the restaurant, so we headed back to the Hailey Hotel. Sure enough, she was at the cashier counter. As I eased by her, I whispered, "I need some info. Please come see me." She nodded as we walked on past.

Talisa and I settled in our room to wait for Betsy. She would have to work us in her schedule, and we didn't know when she would be able to come. I pulled out my notebook and began studying satellite photos and topographical maps that I had of the area around *Black Bear Lodge*. Like Lawson Davis had said, it was pretty rugged. I wasn't sure how to get in there to take a look. But I'd bet a month's wage that Hagan was holed up there.

While I was studying the maps, Talisa went to the bathroom, and to my surprise, she returned with nothing but a towel wrapped around her. When I looked up and noticed her, she let the towel slide to the floor and said, "Don't you think there is something better to do than study those ole maps?" I certainly did!

Several hours later, there was a tap on the door, and as expected, it was Betsy. I told her what we had found out and that we needed to know what she knew about the area. She told us that she really didn't know very much at all. In fact, she didn't even know that Black Bear was owned by a group from Mexico. She added that she lived in the hotel, room 311, in case we needed to talk with her outside of working hours. I told her that was good information to know.

Then we discussed what to do next as it seemed virtually impossible to infiltrate the old resort. Betsy suggested that we first rent a helicopter and do a fly-by. That would give us valuable information, especially if we took some pictures along the way. After we got some pictures and the lay of the place, we could then probably figure out a plan. "What do you really need?" I asked. "Maybe a photo I. D. of Hagan in the compound, or physical contact and recorded conversation with him."

"That would be helpful", she said as she added that I needed enough information to have her people move in and arrest him. She said photos would probably be enough to warrant a raid.

The next day, Talisa and I went to the airport where there was a tourist helicopter service. We told the receptionist what we wanted, and within an hour, a middle-aged man walked up and introduced himself to us and said he would be our pilot. I told him that we really didn't want the tourist ride but that I was interested in looking at the old, closed resorts on Bald Mountain. I went on to explain that I was putting together a story and needed some aerial pictures to help with my report. He told me that should be no problem, and if we would follow him to the landing pad, we'd be up in the air in about ten minutes.

Talisa and I boarded the chopper. I sat in the passenger seat while she got into the back seat. It seemed the pilot was making a last-minute inspection of the helicopter as he circled the aircraft before getting inside. I didn't know if that was a good thing or bad, but he soon boarded and said, "All looks good – ready to go?"

We nodded, and he fired her up and soon lifted off. He took us in the same order that Lawson Davis explained to us. To make my story seem legitimate, I had to view and take pictures of all three lodges. While flying, the pilot hovered over different spots when I asked him. This allowed both Talisa and me to take pictures and jot down some notes. I asked him how we could get to the lodges, and he flew us over the roads that led to the entrances.

Finally, we headed over to Black Bear. As we approached, I jokingly asked him if the lodge was given its name because of the black bears in the area. He said he didn't know but added that there were definitely black bears as well as grizzles around. "Every year or so, we learn of a camper being attacked by a bear. So they are definitely here."

As we flew near, it was very clear that this was a place of privacy. Betsy's description of it as a compound was very appropriate. It was fenced all around with no apparent gate. I even spotted what looked to be an armed guard patrolling the fenced areas. Because of their security, we didn't dare fly too close which meant Talisa had to use a zoom lens to get any detailed pictures. As we flew around, I asked if I could go inside and interview some of the people. The pilot said he didn't know. We spotted two helicopter pads, and it looked as if that was the only way to enter. I then asked him if he would fly me in on another day. He was very hesitant at first but he eventually said he would rather not. I understood his position and accepted it without argument.

I asked the pilot to circle around several times in hopes of spotting a place where he might land outside the compound that was close enough for us to hike in but no such place was found. The mountains were more like rock cliffs, and only an experienced rock climber could scale such walls. There had to be some way to get inside! But if not, maybe we could stake out on top of one of the cliffs with powerful camera equipment that would allow us to take pictures of the inside, and with some luck, we might get a picture of Robert Hagan.

Before leaving the area, I asked the pilot to show me where the old road was that once led to the lodge. He pointed out where it intersected with Park Road 1A, and I thought that might be our starting place.

Later that day, I knocked on Betsy's door as it was her day off. She invited us inside her room. I was eager to share with her what I had found out. We sat around her table in the corner of the room and began by showing her the photos we had taken. She was amazed at how well-fortified *Black Bear* was as she had no idea it had the type of security that we were showing her.

After showing her the pictures, I told her I really didn't see any way into the area without using a helicopter and that our tour pilot didn't want to fly us in. I told her we wondered about trying to use long-range photography from the top of one of the surrounding cliffs. She thought that might work, but it all depended on how close we could get and the detailed quality of the pictures. Then she asked a sobering question. "What if you get caught and Hagan recognizes you?"

Well, I hadn't thought of that because I didn't expect to get caught! But Betsy had a valid point that we needed to consider. If we were to get caught, I would hope Hagan wouldn't recognize me because of my long hair and beard, plus he thinks I am dead. But I also remembered that the deputy in the jail cell had recognized me. "But what if you do and they check your ID and the name Scroggins from Texas raises a flag?" Betsy quizzed. "I don't know," I said. "Any ideas?"

"Well, for one, we need to get you some other identification and an alias. Secondly, we will need to remove any link between you and the FBI, and thirdly we need to have something to give some creditability to your research story."

"How do we do that?" I asked.

Betsy replied by saying, "Let me work on that while I also try to get you a couple of cameras with powerful zoom lens. I will also try to use the agency to get some satellite imagery from within the walls. What I want you to do is to hang around town and do the tourist thing until I get back to you. Deal?"

"Deal," we agreed.

So for the next couple of days, we lounged around the hotel and visited the novelty shops in town. When I was in the room, I kept studying the pictures we had taken of Black Bear (except when Talisa dropped her towel!) In one photo, we had the old ski lift which led from inside the compound to near the top of one of the cliffs. On the backside of that cliff was the former ski slope that led back down into the lodge area, but now the slope was cut off from the lodge by the high perimeter fence. But the lift caught my attention, and I wondered if it still worked and if perhaps that might be a way to get to the lodge. I needed to find out how ski lifts worked. Talisa suggested we go ask Lawson Davis to show us his lift controls, so that afternoon we were on our way to visit Mr. Davis once again.

Fortunately, when we arrived at his lodge, he remembered us and asked how the story was going. I told him that I was still gathering information which was the reason I was seeing him again. I asked him if he could explain to me how the ski lift controls worked. "Is there an operator who stops and starts it, or is it automatic? Can it go backward, or is it only forward-moving?"

Again, he was very willing to help and explained that the lifts were partly automatic. By that, he meant that an operator started and stopped the lift in motion, but it automatically stopped at the top long enough to allow the riders to get off. After one minute, the lift automatically began moving again until the next chair got to the top, and it stopped again for one minute. That continued until the operator stopped the movement.

"What if someone gets hurt or sick or something like that?" Talisa asked.

"The ground-based operator can override the automatic system. Matter of fact, there are three other places along the gondola route where people can override the ground-based operator. This is in place in case of an emergency situation such as you just mentioned. Let's say there was an emergency near the top of the lift and the ground-based operator couldn't see that far, so there is another station near the top that overrides all the other controls."

After telling us about how the lift controls worked, Mr. Davis called a man from maintenance to take us to the control room so that we can observe how it works. We found the process to be fascinating. The control panel had more lights than a 747 along with a large digital display that showed where each seat was and how many people, if any, were in it.

The operator told us that most of the time, his job was simply to sit and watch. He pointed to the start and stop buttons and told us that was his primary job – to start and stop the lift. After that, everything pretty much ran itself.

I asked him what would happen in an emergency situation, and he basically said the same thing that Mr. Davis had told us. He said that if one occurred near the top of the mountain that he couldn't see, three other remote-control rooms could override his controls. I told him the system was very impressive. Before we left, I asked him if the controls for all lifts were similar to this one,

He said, "All the operating ski lifts use this exact same system. The government regulations forced us to standardize our systems for safety reasons. So an operator at one lodge could in cases of emergency be called upon to operate the system at another lodge."

"What about the old abandoned lifts?"

"Well, if they were shut down recently, then the answer is yes. But if they were shut down farther back than five years ago, there were no safety standards then and the systems were not necessarily the same."

Later that evening, Betsy stopped by during her work break. She handed me a large manila envelope that contained some papers and driver's licenses for both Talisa and me.

"Inside the envelope, you will find photo identification for each of you," she said. "Your names are Mr. and Mrs. Richard King from Nashville, Tennessee. We kept the first names the same which will make it easier for you. You will also find some previous reports supposedly written by you along with a request from a major real estate investor asking you to research the feasibly of purchasing abandoned ski resorts. Always keep this information in your possession. Also, keep wearing your recording rings and watches. Tomorrow you are to go to Lou's Photo Shop in Hailey and tell the manager your code name, and he will provide you with the needed photo equipment. After that, you are on your own. If you get some conclusive photos of Hagan, get out of there as fast as possible and hightail it back here. Any questions?"

Neither of us had any questions as things seemed pretty clear to us. We both went to bed that night wondering what tomorrow might bring.

14

Chapter

After Betsy left, Talisa and I were eager to get started but also were a bit nervous. I was excited because I was actually getting ready to gather the information that was needed to have Robert Hagan apprehended and brought to justice. I looked at my new driver's license and was amazed at how authentic it looked. It had my Texas photo on it, but everything else was from Tennessee. I figured I needed to memorize the zip code and street address where I was supposed to live.

I read the reports that were written by Richard King, and they were really good. They were on official-looking paper that sounded authentic. I was intrigued by the request supposedly written by Baxter Real Estate Company asking me to do research on the abandoned ski resorts. The overall package was very impressive.

That night, we went to bed pretty early as we knew tomorrow would be a full day, but I couldn't go to sleep, so I turned on the television. This was the first time it had been on since we arrived four days ago. As I was flipping through the channels, I stumbled across a football game which really caught my interest. Then I was amazed to see that Boise State was playing LSU! I woke Talisa, who was not sound asleep yet, and told her that an LSU game was on the TV.

We were both interested and sat up and got "snuggling fixed" and watched the game. The announcers were giving Logan nothing but praise. I learned that he was leading their conference in rushing yards with a 4.6 average per carry and that he was second in the nation. He was also second in the nation in touchdowns and only two away from the lead.

As we watched him carry the ball, it was like watching him in high school. It took at least three tacklers to bring him down. One of the announcers likened him to Earl Campbell, the former great Houston Oiler. The announcers were joking around and saying LSU only needed one offensive play and that was, "Give it to Logan!"

I learned that LSU was tied with Alabama for the conference lead and they were to play one another in a few weeks. What a thrill it was to see Logan making such an impact! I whispered to Talisa, "I knew he would! I just knew it!"

The next morning, we were up early and eating in the restaurant. To our surprise, Betsy joined us. She reminded us that we would be on our own and that we were to contact her as soon as we got back. If we failed to check with her, she would assume something was wrong and would act accordingly. She also told us that our watch recorder transmissions were limited to only a few miles, so it would be unlikely if anyone was close enough to monitor our signals. But if the agent's receivers should get within range and begin picking up our signal, the underside of the watch would silently vibrate for about three seconds. "So if you feel the vibration, you will know that you are being received," she said as she got up from our table and walked away.

After breakfast, we headed to the camera shop and picked up our photography equipment. It was heavier than I expected, and I was concerned about having to climb rugged terrain with it. I figured time would tell if I could do it or not. There was a hiking store across the street from the camera shop, and we made our way over there and bought backpacks for Talisa and me. I figured they would be helpful as we made our hike into the mountains.

As we drove up State Park 1, I was looking for the abandoned road that led up to Black Bear. It was a beautiful drive, but I was more focused on finding the road than enjoying the scenery. We passed by what I believed to be the roads that led to the two private lodges before getting to Black Bear. The first of the two had a sign on the side of the road with an arrow pointing and said, "Prudential Insurance Recreational Facility." What I thought to be the road leading up to the San Diego Padres lodge simply had a "private road" sign at the entrance. But I was looking for the Black Bear road. I had driven what I felt was a sufficient distance to have intersected it. I wondered if I had missed it even though I was carefully looking for it. I told Talisa that I'd drive another mile or two and then we'd turn around and retrace our tracks. Just as soon as I said that, I spotted a road ahead that looked to be the one we wanted. When we got to it, there was a barricade across it with a sign that said, "Road Closed." This had to be our road!

I drove around the barricade and headed up a road that obviously had not been maintained. There were potholes from the harsh winters, tree saplings growing right next to the pavement edges, and a few were growing out of potholes right in the middle of the road. I had to maneuver the jeep around and through the maze as if we were driving through an obstacle course. A few times it was necessary to shift down into four-wheel-drive to get across some logs or other debris that was across the road. We drove for about two miles up and around the rugged mountain terrain before we encountered the mudslide, which was now covered with forest vegetation. It was here that we stopped the jeep.

I filled my backpack with camera equipment and binoculars while Talisa put sandwiches and snacks and bottled water in hers. I also put all my papers and notes in the smaller zip-locked pouch on the side of her pack. We crossed over the mudslide, which was probably at least half a mile wide, before getting back to the road surface. After we got back on the road, our hike was much easier. We stopped frequently to rest and for me to change carrying arms for the heavy camera. Nearly an hour later, we were on a peak overlooking the compound. I thought about the Marty Robbins song, *El Paso,* as the cowboy was on the hill overlooking the city below.

I set the big camera on a tripod, and when I got it focused, I was amazed at how clear everything was. I told Talisa this was just like being inside the compound. I began snapping pictures. Since it was digital, there was basically an unlimited number of pictures that I could take. From where we were, I could only see the lower part of the ski lift, but I got some good pictures of it.

We watched for quite a while and soon figured out where the main building was by the number of people who kept going in and out. I took a few pictures of men around that building, but no Hagan. I was beginning to have doubts that he was there. All that morning I didn't see any signs of Hagan. I chuckled to myself as I remembered what Grandpa would have said. He'd say, "I ain't seen hide nor hair of 'im."

It was a clear sunny day, and before long, we were coming out of the coats we were wearing. Although the temperature was in the thirties, it didn't seem anywhere close to how cold mid-thirties felt back home. I guess the high altitude made the difference.

As we were eating a sandwich, I heard a helicopter approaching. We watched as it circled the compound and finally landed on one of the helicopter pads. I quickly found it in my camera lens and saw four men come out of the headquarters and meet with the pilot. After a few minutes of conversation, one of the men called another man into the group. He pointed in our direction and immediately scurried back into the headquarters building. Then the four men boarded the helicopter and lifted off and flew directly over us.

I wondered if they had spotted us or if they were so busy in conversation that they never looked out the windows. I finished my sandwich, and Talisa and I were talking about what a beautiful day it was. I mentioned that when we got back to the hotel, I needed to call home to let Dad and Janet know that we were still alive and well. Then suddenly, and with no warning, we were surrounded by a band of Mexican men pointing rifles toward us! I was scared, and from the look in Talisa's eyes, she was too. One of them motioned for me to stand up, which we both did. Then they led us away without ever saying a word. I was glad Talisa could speak Spanish in case they started talking to us. Others grabbed our gear and backpacks. We were led down the rugged mountains toward the compound. As we got near the perimeter fence, we stopped, and one of the men talked in Spanish into his radio and a door opened up that exposed a tunnel into the mountain. After we had entered the tunnel, the door closed behind us. I wondered if this was going to be our burial tomb.

After a short distance, we got on an elevator that took us down inside a building that I presumed was the headquarters. We were ushered into an office where a man who had a look of authority stood from behind his desk. I was glad when he spoke to us in English.

As he stood, he gave a hand motion, and the entourage of armed soldiers left the room, which left us with just the leader and three others in the room.

'Ah, my friends, I am Cap-a-tan Lopez. This is my home, and I was curious as to why you were invading my privacy with your expensive cameras."

I removed my wallet and handed him my ID and told him that my wife and I had been hired by a real estate investment firm in Nashville to research abandoned ski lodges. "We were able to get to all the other lodges, but we could find no way to enter yours, so I had to improvise. We mean you no harm. If you will look inside my wife's backpack, you will find information confirming my story."

When I said that, he motioned for one of his men to fetch the backpack, and he pulled out the papers. He saw information and notes that I had jotted down about the other lodges along with my maps. He read the letter I had from *Baxter Real Estate Company* which seemed to satisfy him that I was telling the truth. But all of a sudden, he called the telephone number at the bottom of the letter and asked to speak to the person who had signed the letter. I could only hear his end of the conversation as he asked if a Richard King was assigned by their firm to research ski lodges. There was a brief silence, and my heart was revving up to overdrive. Finally, Cap-a-tan thanked the man and hung up his phone. He looked me in the eye and said our stories matched, but he had to be sure I was telling the truth.

After that, his demeanor changed, and he welcomed us as his guests. He even agreed to an interview to answer my questions about the advantages of purchasing a lodge as an investment. I didn't ask anything about his particular operation, and we kept the conversation strictly about investments and the liabilities and risks that could be expected from such a purchase.

As we talked, I kept watching men coming and going into and away from the building, and occasionally one would poke his head into the office and say something in Spanish. A few times when this happened, Cap-a-tan invited them in and introduced us. As I was getting to the point where I had no more questions, I was beginning to wonder how we were going to get out of here. Just before I asked him, the unexpected happened! Robert Hagan popped in, and he was invited to come in for an introduction.

As he walked toward us, he looked directly at me, and I only hoped my change in appearance was enough of a disguise to keep him from recognizing me. Cap-a-tan introduced us as Mr. and Mrs. Richard King from Tennessee. Hagan said it was a pleasure meeting us, and then asked, as he looked at me, "Have we met before? You seem familiar to me."

Disguising my voice, I replied, "I don't know. Have you spent much time around Nashville?" All the while, I was snapping pictures with my ring and only hoped Talisa was recording. "Now, what was your name again?"

"Robert Hagan, and no, I have never been to Nashville. Have you ever been to Louisiana? "

"Yes, I went to New Orleans once during Mardi Grau, and man was that a wild place!" We both chuckled, and then he dropped the matter, which was fine with me.

While we were talking, Talisa jumped. I asked her what was wrong and she replied that it was just another one of the twitches that she sometimes has. I knew from what she said that her watch had vibrated. Help was nearby!

As he was leaving the room, I jokingly asked, "Hey, Robert, are you related to Festus Hagan on the ole Gun *Smoke* westerns?" I said that for the benefit of new ears listening in to let them know that Robert Hagan was there, and they should have a picture of him taken with my ring camera.

"Naw, I guess not, but we do spell our last names alike."

After he left, I got back to my interview and told Cap-a-tan that I had all the information I needed and asked if he could show us the way out.

"Out? Oh no, Senor! You and your lovely wife are my guests, and I expect you to stay at least one night with us. After all, we are not used to having such a lovely senora among us. I will have you escorted to your quarters, and we will come and get you for dinner tonight."

He snapped his fingers, and one of the men standing in the back of the room immediately motioned us out of the room and took us to one of the rooms in the old ski lodge. When we were inside, I heard the door lock behind us as our escort left. I had mixed emotions. On one hand, I felt our story was accepted and the man didn't feel threatened. But on the other hand, I was uneasy because of Hagan being here plus the fact that we were locked in a room with no apparent way out. However, there were some windows that let us see outside, and if we wanted to, I suppose we could jump from our second-floor window to the ground. Still, I hoped we wouldn't need to do that. Talisa and I verbally discussed our situation and where we were so as to give the FBI agents information if they should be listening.

While looking out the window, I saw Hagan rush into the headquarters building. Not long afterward, he and Cap-a-tan came out together and were making their way toward our building at a rather brisk pace, and I didn't like it. I was fearful that Hagan had figured out who I was. Soon I heard someone unlocking our door, and I knew who it was. They came into our room and Hagan said, "Scroggins, I thought you were dead!"

"Scroggins? What do you mean?" I replied.

"It took me a while, but something about you kept gnawing at me. I felt I knew you from somewhere, and then it hit me. You are Richard Scroggins!"

I played ignorant about what he was saying and insisted to Cap-a-tan that this man must be loco. I again showed him my identification and insisted that I was Richard King.

At that instant, we were interrupted by the sound of helicopters landing. Cap-a-tan Lopez rushed over to the window and immediately cried out, "It's the Feds!" He pointed to Talisa and me and ordered, "Grab them and take 'em with us!"

Hagan grabbed Talisa and me by our arms and pushed us forward as we were following Lopez in what was almost a run. When we got to the base of the stairs, I pulled away and slugged Hagan, knocking him loose from Talisa, and we took off running across the courtyard. By this time, it was sheer chaos! Mexicans were heading in all directions along with three helicopters that were each unloading at least five FBI agents. Soon gunfire opened up as both sides took cover. Talisa and I raced for the ski lift control room while Hagan and Lopez took cover inside the lodge.

Fortunately, the door was unlocked, and we darted inside. It looked a lot like the control room that Lawson Davis had shown us, but nothing was powered up. The display was dark, and all the panel lights were off. I only hoped that the lift would still work if I could get power to it. I looked for a master power switch but found none. There must be some kind of control switch! While I was searching, Talisa whispered that Hagan was making his way toward us. We were able to slip behind the display unit and only hoped that Hagan wouldn't be able to find us.

Then the door swung open, and he quickly looked inside. As he did, there was a barrage of bullets pounding the building wall which forced him to duck low and race for better cover. When he left, I eased out from hiding and pushed the door closed. When I closed the door, I noticed a circuit breaker panel behind the door. I don't know why I hadn't seen that earlier. I didn't have time to figure out which breaker went with what, so I turned them all on, and when I did, all the displays lit up like a Christmas tree.

I stood in front of the control board and pushed the start button, and to my joy, the gondola started moving! I rushed Talisa out the side door and into a seat. I told her to get off at the top and wait for me. When she was seated, it took off. I had planned to get on the next seat, but before I could do so, I was jumped from behind. Hagan had come back! He landed a blow to my right temple which took me to the ground. Then he pulled out a knife and said this was going to be the end of me as I felt the knife go deep into my rib cage. As I fell to the floor, I saw Hagan get into the next lift seat and rise toward the cliff above.

I finally managed to get to my feet and pull myself into the next seat which was at least ten seats behind Hagan, and maybe more. I had to struggle to stay in my seat and had it not been for the safety bar, I probably would have fallen out, which likely would have been fatal since I was a hundred feet or more above the ground.

I had to hang on in order to protect Talisa. If she was at the top of the cliff waiting for me, she would be easy prey for Hagan. He could take her and use her as leverage for his safety. As I got near the top, I realized the shooting had stopped below. Finally, my seat was at the top and the gondola stopped for what I knew to be only a minute. I had to get my safety bar raised and out of the seat, or else I would have to make the return trip back to the ground station. It was a struggle, as I felt faint, but I finally managed to fall out into the snow face down.

My midsection hurt, and when I tried to stand, I noticed the snow was covered with my blood. That was the last thing I remembered until I was on a gurney being carried back down the mountain. I had to stop them! Talisa was still out there as well as Hagan!

"Hey!" I cried out. The men carrying me stopped and wanted to know what was wrong. I told them I had to find my wife as she was out there someplace. They told me to stay calm and that their agents would find her. They would not listen to reason. My bleeding had stopped, and I was well bandaged. I wanted to go look for Talisa, but they would not hear of it.

When we were back inside the compound, they made me lie down in one of the guest rooms at the lodge while the other agents were searching every building. They gave me a shot of something for pain, and at that very moment, I felt as good as I ever had. While lying down, a thousand things ran through my head. Finally, I asked one of my two caretakers if he could go find me a cup of coffee, and while he was gone, I jumped the other agent by surprise and overpowered him and escaped. I was protected somewhat by the cover of darkness, and I HAD to make it back up the mountain to find Talisa! The only thing I knew to do was to get back on the ski lift again.

I carefully made my way back to the control room without detection, and fortunately, the gondola was still running. I jumped into the next seat, and up, up, and away I went!

15

Chapter

It seemed like forever before the lift made it to the top of the cliff where I unloaded. Although it was night, the moon was full, and I could see very clearly. I noticed there were tracks in the snow going in all directions near the lift. Some were small while others were larger. It was as if Talisa had been prancing around waiting for me. As I expanded my search, I spotted what I presumed to be her tracks heading across the mountain ridge, and the larger tracks, which I knew were Hagan's, headed in the same direction.

It didn't take an Indian scout to figure out that he was on her trail! I only hoped I could find her before he did. I raced through the silence of the cold night air tracking both sets of footprints through the crusty snow. I wasn't sure, but I thought we were going west. And if I remembered my maps correctly, there was nothing in this direction for at least twenty miles.

I had to stop every little bit to catch my breath as I was not used to the high altitude plus my side was beginning to bleed again from my running and stretching the muscles of my abdomen. While I was making one of my stops, I heard a helicopter in the distance that sounded like it was getting closer. I knew it would be hard to see because the area was mostly concealed by timber. But I had no fear of the chopper as I assumed those men were on my side and were trying to help me.

I had resumed my fast-paced trailing when the helicopter hovered over me with a bright spotlight surrounding me. I stopped and waved. Since it was too rugged for the chopper to land, two agents were lowered down with a rescue basket. The agents insisted that I get into the basket and then into the chopper. I argued against doing so and explained to them that Hagan was stalking my wife and that I was following their trail in the snow.

One of the agents said they knew about that, and for now, she was alright, although Hagan had overtaken her. I wanted to know how they knew, and he reminded me about her recording watch. They had been listening to her all along and were about to move in and rescue her when I got in the way. Then he said forcefully, "Get into the basket and let us do our job!"

Once I was inside the helicopter, I could also listen to Talisa talking. She was making it clear that Hagan had forced her into some kind of rock overhang or small cave for the night. He was saying that she was his ticket out of there, and as long as he felt that way, I thought she would be safe.

Occasionally, we would lose her signal, but as we circled around, it was soon restored. I knew that each time we regained the signal, her watch would vibrate and alert her that we were nearby.

We kept flying around the area, but never spotted them, although we frequently saw the two agents on the ground following the snow tracks. I knew that since Hagan and Talisa had stopped, the agents would eventually overtake them.

The helicopter crew was in radio communication with the agents on the ground as well as listening to Talisa. We kept circling around where we thought they should be. By this time, my pain-killing shot was beginning to wear off and my pain was severe, but I dared not say a word for fear they would take me back to the compound and postpone the search.

Then we heard Talisa say, "Look, Hagan, I see some men coming this way. You ought to know that you can't get away."

"I can as long as I have your pretty face with me!" he said, and it sounded like he was getting to his feet. Then we heard Talisa let out a small scream as if he had hit her, and then the communication stopped. All we heard was occasional muffled background noise.

The chief told the ground agents that they were getting close and to use caution. "We certainly don't want a dead victim or agents. Since communication from Talisa had stopped, we didn't know if Hagen tore her watch away or if he was just making her quiet so as not to expose their location. The chief decided that he needed to be on the ground. He radioed to the men on the ground, "Hold your ground and don't force his hand. I'll be there soon." Then, he instructed the pilot to hover while he was lowered in the basket to the ground. I begged and pleaded to go with him, and he finally consented if I promised to stay out of the way and let them do their job.

Within a few minutes, we were on the ground, but we didn't know exactly where they were, although their snow tracks were pretty easy to follow. The agent in charge, with his pistol drawn, cried out, "Hagan! This is federal agent Kinsley. Don't be stupid! Think it through - you kill the girl, and then what? You are an open target with nowhere to go. It's over. Lay down your weapon, and it will be easier for all concerned. There is no reason for anyone to get hurt!"

There was not a sound from anyone. Were they still there, or were they again on the run? Should we move forward at the risk of Hagen killing Talisa, or should we hold back and be cautious? After a few minutes of waiting, Agent Kinsley motioned for the other two agents to ease around in opposite directions in hopes of spotting them. If they saw them, they were to click the transmitter on their radio twice. The chief and I held our ground watching and waiting. Finally, we started to ease along the trail of the footprints, but we saw no sign of the two of them. We continued to slowly ease along. By this time, I was holding my side and the bleeding was really beginning to be obvious. The chief agent noticed my condition and said I needed to return to the compound and get some attention.

I assured him that I was good to keep moving and that there was no way I was going back and leave my wife in the hands of Hagan. Approximately fifteen minutes later, we got to a crevice in the cliff that appeared to be where they were holed up. We cautiously approached, and when we got closer, I saw Talisa lying on the ground off to one side. She was bound and gagged. Apparently, Hagan had cut the sleeves out of his shirt and ripped them to make ties and tied her up and left. I untied her and she hugged me so tightly, but when I flinched, she said, "Oh, Richard! You're hurt!"

I told her I was, but that was not as important as getting her back safely. She told the agent that Hagan slugged her when the agents were getting close and apparently made a run for it after he tied her up. "I guess he figured his odds were better alone than with me slowing him down," she said.

We didn't know where he was, but he probably had at least a thirty-minute head start.

Since Talisa was safe and my bleeding was getting worse, Agent Kinsley ordered that we be flown back to the lodge where we would spend the night and regroup tomorrow. Several agents were left behind to track Hagan while the helicopter flew us back to the compound. I thought it should be easy for them to follow his tracks in the snow.

As soon as we touched down, the two previous caregivers were there to meet us and ushered us back to the room where I had been earlier, and I promised that I would give them no trouble this time because I had the love of my life back with me.

The next morning, the chief agent came to our room and asked how I was feeling, and I told him that I was still in some pain, but not as bad as last night. "Mr. Scroggins, you have done an admirable job in smoking out Robert Hagan. We didn't have the men available to do what you did, and you were willing to risk your life in order to accomplish this mission. My men followed him last night as he circled back toward the compound. Eventually, he got back to where there were a lot of other snow tracks heading in all directions, and they lost him. So, you need to be especially vigilant. We don't know if he knows that you are still alive but be on the alert just in case he tries something. But let me tell you what else you did. You broke up perhaps the largest smuggling ring in our country. Lopez and his men were extremely active and hopefully, your evidence will help put them away."

"What evidence?" I wondered and asked.

"Before we raided the compound, we found your camera back on the ridge. We sent it to the FBI lab in Denver and received word back last night that the four men getting on the helicopter were heads of the four largest drug gangs in Central America. We assume they were working a deal with Lopez to move their drugs into this country. He seemed to recognize them and has probably worked with them often."

I was amazed at what I was hearing not to mention the potential danger I was getting into. I remember Dad telling me how ruthless the drug cartels were. I told agent Kinsley that I thought Hagan was smuggling pelts and alligator skins when he was in Louisiana. He explained that Lopez ran a smuggling organization and would move any product if the money was good enough. "We suspect that he smuggled drugs, animals, young women, guns, etc. You name it, and if there was money in it, he was willing to move it."

He explained that Lopez and his men were contained in a jail that was on the compound and should be moved later today to a proper facility.

"I wanted to thank you for your courageous involvement in helping break up this ring and to tell you to keep an eye on your back. I will need you to write up a report about what happened. Just write in your own words what has taken place over the past few days. Any questions?" he asked.

"Yes Sir, just one. How did you know to invade?"

He smiled and said, "Lopez clued us when he called to verify your credentials. The phone number on the papers was to our Denver office, and our people were instructed how to respond if a call came in on that line. So we knew where you were and figured you would not be able to get out. Then we got close enough to receive your transmission, and after listening to some of your conversations, we concluded that your life was in danger, so we put together a team to invade and rescue."

I told him I was very thankful for his help. As he was about to leave, he laid some paper and a ballpoint pen on the table, but before he got to the door, one of the agents rushed in and said, "Sir! Lopez and his men have escaped! There is a secret passage inside the cell that leads to a tunnel beneath the floor. We don't know where they are or how long they've been gone!"

Agent Kinsley rushed out of the room without saying another word to me and closed the door behind him.

Talisa and I looked at each other in amazement and wondered where Lopez was, and more seriously, we wondered if he had hooked up with Hagan and if they would come after us. I went to the table to start writing my report, but I had a hard time consecrating on it. I got about halfway into it when the agents returned and escorted Talisa and me to the helicopter and flew us to the regional hospital in Boise. They told me that the agency would take care of returning the rented equipment along with the Jeep that was left on the mountain road.

When we got to the hospital, I was taken to the emergency room for the doctors to look at my knife wound. They took x-rays which thankfully showed no damage was done to any vital organs, but the knife wound was very deep. The medical staff cleaned it and trimmed away the outer skin near the surface that had already begun to die. I figured they would stitch me up and let me go, but not true. Since the wound was deep, the doctor said it needed to heal from the inside out, which meant it was to remain an open wound. During the next several weeks, I was to keep a clean bandage on it and keep it flushed with antibiotic-type liquids. To my amazement, the doctor actually suggested that I use hydrogen peroxide that could be bought at the grocery store.

The worst part was that the doctor said I had to see him regularly because his biggest concern was an infection. He said if the wound got infected, it could lead to major surgery to remove the infected area as well as any other parts of the body where the infection might spread. I explained to him that I lived in Texas and really needed to get back home. He was opposed to any kind of travel plus he said he figured I would get back to Texas and not go for regular check-ups, and I must admit that thought had definitely crossed my mind. We finally compromised. He conceded if I'd stay in Idaho for a week, and if the wound seemed to be healing, he would dismiss me to a doctor in Dallas.

I had to stay in the hospital for one night primarily for observation. Talisa was allowed to stay with me, and they brought in a cot where she could sleep. Later that day, to our surprise, Betsy and Agent Kinsley stopped by to visit me. It was good to see familiar faces, and they seemed almost like family. They wanted to know how we were doing and what my prognosis was. They were also concerned about Talisa and the ordeal she had been through. She assured them that she was doing okay even though she had been very scared and that she had a nightmare about it last night. They told her that was probably to be expected as she feared for her life. I told them about the things that had happened to me, and then Agent Kinsley wanted to talk business.

"Richard, you showed a lot of loyalty and bravery the last few days in what you did. I commend you for that, but I also want to fuss at you a little bit too. Hagan is still on the run, and as far as we can tell, he is nowhere around the compound. We found what looked to be snowmobile tracks on the next ridge, and we suspect he used his cell phone and notified someone to come in from the backside to rescue him. Now in all likelihood, that could have been avoided if you had held your position in the compound. If you had never activated the gondola, he probably would have been apprehended, maybe even killed by the raid as six others were. If you had found a place for safe hiding and let my men do their job, the outcome could have been different, and you would probably not be in the hospital."

"Yes, sir. But you need to understand that I was simply trying to get myself and my wife to a safe place away from the raid. We were trying to get out of the way so as not to interfere with you and your men doing their job, but Hagan interrupted me and messed everything up. I regret that he got away, and I'm sorry you feel that I hampered your invasion, but if I had it to do over again, I'd probably do the same thing because, in the heat of the moment, it seemed to me to be the only thing to do."

Kinsley smiled and replied, "I believe you would. Truthfully, if I had been in your shoes, I'd probably have done the same thing." Then he handed me a bag that contained a few things Betsy had brought us from our hotel room. There were some welcomed hygiene items along with a change of clothes for Talisa and me. We expressed our gratitude to her.

Betsy said that we should return to stay at the hotel until we left for Texas. I told her I was hoping that would be in about a week. Then she pulled my cell phone out of her purse! She said one of the agents found it on the ground near the surveillance camera. He figured I must have dropped it when we were apprehended.

Before they left, both of them reminded us again about being alert for not only Hagan, but also for some of Lopez's men. Since I had basically shut down their western operation and six of their men had been killed, they might feel they needed to settle the score. Agent Kinsley asked me if I felt that we needed around-the-clock protection. I told him I had not even considered that and didn't know. "What do you think?" I asked. He suggested that it was better to be safe than sorry, and even though they were short-handed, he'd have someone stationed outside my door while I was at the hospital. After they left, I called home and spoke to Dad. It was good to hear his voice, and he was thrilled to hear mine. I told him that we were alright, but that I had a little accident and was in the hospital but should be getting out tomorrow and hopefully coming home next week. I told him not to worry and that I'd explain everything when we got home. Naturally, he had many questions but was content to table them until he saw me. He was thankful that we were alright and said they wouldn't worry as much as they had been.

The next day, I was released from the hospital, and the agent who had been watching my door drove us to the Hailey Hotel.

A cold front had moved in, and it was snowing big time. I was glad that I wasn't driving and even more glad that we weren't still deep in the mountain wilderness. When we got to the hotel, it actually felt a little bit like home. Talisa and I both had gotten acquainted with some of the staff, and as we walked in, they all greeted us like long-time friends. Betsy was at her counter and gave a little half wave and a smile to let us know that she saw us.

We got settled into our room and pulled back the drapes so we could watch it snow. I had seen more snow than Talisa, but it was still beautiful to watch. The flakes were not as huge in size as some that I had seen, but they were certainly big enough to see, and it was falling so heavily that we could not see the stores across the street. We took advantage of the romantic atmosphere and enjoyed our honeymoon time together.

Later that day, Betsy stopped by to check on us and gave us a two-way radio in case she needed to get in touch with me. Although she didn't mention it, I knew she was still concerned about our safety. I asked her who was "on watch" when she was off duty, and she said, "The other girl at the counter is also an agent plus the two clerks at the registration desk. Between the four of us, we keep a pretty close watch over things." I thanked her for being our watchdog. I told her I felt like a VIP with secret service men around. She smiled and said, "Richard, you are a VIP," which made me feel good.

For the next several days, I tried to take it easy and Talisa was getting more proficient in tending to my wound. When I looked at it, it didn't seem to be getting any better. I wasn't sure the doctor knew what he was talking about when he said we needed to leave it open so it could heal from the inside out.

Finally, it was the day before I was to see the doctor and hopefully get permission to return to Texas. We were kicked back watching television when I received a call on my two-way radio. Betsy said in a frantic-sounding voice, "Richard, do not open your door for any reason! A Mexican stranger just got on the elevator. It may be nothing, but let's take no chances. I'll alert hotel security."

Talisa hid in the small closet while I was looking out the "peep-hole" in the door. My heart was pounding and my palms and forehead began to sweat as I saw a man standing in front of our door. He stood there for a few minutes before finally knocking and saying "Room Service." By this time, I had moved into the bathroom and radioed Betsy that he was in the hallway and knocking on our door.

16
Chapter

Since I didn't go to the door, there was another knock, but this time it was harder and more forceful. While I was trying to decide what I would do if he was able to get inside, I heard a loud scream from the hall. Soon, thereafter I could hear a lot of activity going on out there, and I heard someone cry out, "Call 911!"

I looked back through the peephole and did not see the man. Instead, I saw several people scurrying past. I felt it was safe to open the door, and when I did, I saw a hotel security officer lying in a pool of blood in the hall. I rushed over to get a closer look, and by this time emergency personnel were arriving. I overheard one of the paramedics say that he was still alive but had lost a lot of blood. They soon had him on a gurney and into the elevator.

By this time, Betsy was on the scene and concluded that the man was after me, and when the security officer questioned him, he had a silencer on his pistol and shot him before escaping down the stairway. "At least, we assume he escaped. He may still be in the hotel on some other floor. Richard, I can't stress enough the need for you to be careful."

Talisa joined us and said, "Richard, I'm scared. We need to get back to Texas pronto." I had to agree with her and said softly under my breath, "If I had only listened to Dad and left finding

Hagan alone, then I would not be wounded, and this man would not be shot. Maybe one day, I'll learn to heed his wisdom."

The rest of the day was without incident. The hotel was filled with investigators and news reporters. I tried to avoid them all, especially the news media. The last thing I needed was for my face to be flashed on local television. Finally, things settled down and the hall was clear of all the people. The only thing left to remind us of what happened was the blood stain on the carpet. I figured the carpet would have to be replaced in order to get rid of the stain.

Later in the evening, Betsy brought supper to our room. She also brought along a picture of the man entering the elevator and wanted to know if we recognized him. I looked closely and thought I did. "He looks like one of the men who were in the room with us when we talked with Lopez."

Talisa added, "I definitely recognize him. If you look closely, you can see that he has a scar under his right eye. He is the one I overheard Lopez telling in Spanish to lock us up and keep us secured."

So, we concluded that Lopez was out to settle the score. I wondered how they found us, and Betsy reminded me that it was easy to call around to see if a Richard Scroggins or Richard King was registered in the hotel. The same thing could be said about air flights. A simple telephone call can get you a wealth of information. In some instances, you don't even need a telephone call if you have computer access. I was now wishing I had registered under another name. I decided that when the doctor released me to go home, I would book our flight in the name of Richard King and not Scroggins.

I didn't sleep very well that night as I was aware of every sound. It seemed that each time I dozed off, the heater would cycle on and wake me up. But sometime in the middle of the night, I must have fallen asleep because I was awakened by the bright morning sun shining into our room. We were soon up and eating breakfast in the lobby restaurant as we waited for our pre-arranged driver to take us to the Boise Regional Hospital for my check-up and hopefully my release.

After we had finished eating, Talisa and I sat at our table drinking a second cup of coffee when I saw a man walk up to the front desk, and the clerk pointed in our direction. The man turned and walked toward us. I was skeptical now and wondered if he was a friend or foe. As he approached, he introduced himself and said he had been instructed to drive us to Boise. I still wondered if I could trust him or if he was one of Lopez's hitmen. I really didn't have any reason not to trust him, but now everyone seemed suspicious.

As it turned out, he was a legitimate agent and we arrived at the hospital on time and without incident. I met with the doctor, and after he looked at my wound, he said it looked to be healing as expected and that I should come back to see him in about three weeks. I reminded him about our discussion about me going back to Texas. He said he had forgotten about that, but then he said, "I see no reason for you not to go back home if you fly and don't try to drive. Driving that far would stress the wound but flying shouldn't be too bad." Then, he said he would call and transfer my records to a Doctor Stansell at the Baylor Hospital in Dallas. I should report to him in three weeks for a follow-up check. He looked at Talisa next and said, "Young lady, keep up your good work in caring for his wound. None of my staff could have done any better." We thanked him and left.

As soon as I got back to the hotel, I told Betsy how things went and asked if she thought it was alright for me to book a flight home for tomorrow. She thought that would be fine, and if I could get a morning flight, she would be able to drive us to the airport.

I was able to book us on an early morning Delta flight from Boise nonstop to Dallas DFW. I called and told Dad that we should be in Dallas at about 1:30 and in Tyler at about 4:00 p.m. He said someone would be there to pick us up. Just before I hung up, I remembered to tell him that we were flying under the name of Mr. and Mrs. Richard King.

Early the next morning, Betsy drove us to the local airport, and it was really sad to tell her goodbye. I felt that we had developed a close friendship. I invited her to come to visit us if she was ever in East Texas, and she promised that she would. We soon boarded our commuter plane to Boise where we made our way to the Delta terminal.

We had a brief delay before boarding the plane, so I went to the gift shop and noticed one of the feature stories on the cover of the *Sports Illustrated Magazine* was entitled, "The Freshman Sensation at LSU." I naturally bought the magazine to read during our flight. Soon, we were aboard and Talisa wanted the window seat, which was fine with me. While we were waiting to taxi away, and just before they closed the doors, my heart almost stopped beating. One of the last passengers to board the plane was Robert Hagan! As he passed by our seat, he nodded and said, "Scroggins, you're hard to get rid of. Have a nice flight," as he walked on toward the rear of the plane. I pulled out my cell phone to call the number Albert Jennings had given me, but of all times, my battery only had one bar and the light was blinking. I knew it was about to go dead. I dialed the number anyway, but before anyone could answer, my phone died. I could not believe this! Talisa hadn't charged her phone since before the "incident", so we knew hers was dead.

Thoughts raced through my mind at ninety miles per hour. Should I tell the flight attendant that a criminal was on board? If I did, and he was confronted, would he shoot her and the entire plane? It would be like him to do something like that. Should I just keep quiet until we got to Dallas? Did he know we were on this flight or was it a coincidence that we were on the same plane? Was he monitoring my phone, or worse yet, was Dad's line being tapped? Did he have plans to attack me in Dallas or Tyler? Was he going to high jack this plane to Mexico, or worse, explode it like the Middle East terrorists had done? Should I go confront him while we were in the air, or try to ignore that he was on board? Was he playing mind games with me? I looked at Talisa for answers, and she looked frantic and scared. I figured ole Hagan was sitting back in his seat having a big laugh at our expense. Now the hunter became the hunted - the pursuer was the pursued.

The flight took a little over three hours, and it was, without a doubt, the most uneasy three hours of my life. When we landed, Talisa and I got off the plane before Hagan and headed for the American Eagle terminal to catch the plane that would take us to Tyler. I was very uneasy. I kept a close watch over my shoulder as well as at every blind corner. I was expecting Hagan to make his move at any moment.

We made it to our terminal without incident and had to wait for a little over an hour before time to board the plane to Tyler. There was no sign of Hagan. "Where is he?" I asked Talisa. In some respects, I would rather see him than not know where he is. It was the fear of the unknown that bothered me. I was really uneasy and felt strongly that we shouldn't get on that plane to Tyler. I made the decision that we should not.

I went to one of the food court places and paid for a cup of coffee with a ten-dollar bill so I could get some change. I still couldn't believe my cell phone was dead! I went to the payphone and called Albert Jennings. He was not available, so I gave the message to one of his office staff members that Hagen had been on the same plane with us, but I had no idea what had happened to him since we landed in Dallas.

I then used the pay phone to call Dad to see if he could come and get us at DFW rather than Tyler. He said he could and was glad that I called because he was planning to leave for Tyler in about ten minutes. After making that call, Talisa and I went to the farthest corner of the terminal to wait for him to arrive. We kept our backs to the wall so that anyone approaching us would have to come from the front. We didn't have to go to the baggage claim area since all we had was carry-on luggage which made it a lot easier to have changed our minds about going to Tyler.

After some time had passed, the commuter plane left for Tyler, and I felt a little bit easier about Hagan not being around as I felt like he may have been on that plane. I realized I should have watched when we got off the plane to see if he also got off, but I was too scared to stand around and watch. If I had been by myself, I probably would have done so, but I also had the life of Talisa to think about. I wondered if he stayed on the plane and was going to Atlanta. I really felt that he was on the plane to Tyler and that he would have followed us wherever we went. Feeling a bit more comfortable, I pulled out the *Sports Illustrated Magazine* and started reading about Logan and the outstanding accomplishments he had made. I'd read a little and then glance at the clock, read some more, and glance at the clock. This went on for almost an hour when an announcement came over the airport intercom speakers. "May we have your attention, please? We regret to tell you that we have just received word that the American Eagle flight number 114 that was going to Tyler has crashed. We have no information regarding causalities. The cause of the crash is unknown at this time. We will update you as information is forthcoming. Thank you."

I felt numb all over. "Talisa, did you hear that? That was the flight we were supposed to have been on! If we had taken that flight, there is a good possibility that we would be dead right now."

She said, "Richard, do you think Hagan caused it?"

I hadn't thought about that, but now I felt almost certain that he was responsible. I wondered if he had planted a bomb or if he was also on the plane and ended his own life as well. If he caused the crash to try to get me, he had a very warped and cruel mind to take so many innocent lives just to settle the score with me. Then again, human life had never seemed to have much value to Hagan. For the first time, I began to wonder about him as a person. I wondered what kind of childhood he had that had caused him to be so calloused and cruel to others. I wondered if he was married or had a family. I wondered if anyone had ever talked to him about Jesus and becoming a Christian. I somehow suspected he had purposely gone down with the plane.

About an hour later, Dad and Janet walked into the terminal and Talisa spotted them first. What a thrill it was to see them again! We hugged as Dad said, "Have you heard the news?"

"About the crash?" I asked.

He said yes and that he was so thankful that we weren't on that plane. I told him that I just had a very strong feeling that we shouldn't get on it, and now we're so grateful for that decision. We talked about it more as we walked to their car in the parking lot. On the way home, Talisa and I told them all about what happened in Idaho and how Hagan boarded the same plane we were on. I told him I tried to call Jennings, but my phone was dead and that I had merely left a message with his secretary when we got to the airport. I could tell this news was making Dad nervous. Although he didn't say so, I knew he was afraid I had brought serious trouble to East Texas and sad to say, I thought he might be right. Before we got home, Dad called Albert Jennings and set up an appointment for tomorrow morning. I knew he was worried and was thinking to himself, "If only that boy had listened to me!"

Before we got home, the news came on the radio with confirmation that all twenty-five people on board American Flight 114 had died in the crash. There had been no survivors. My heart ached and deep down I felt responsible. Was Hagen one of them?

What a great feeling it was to finally get back home even though there was a cloud of sadness in the air. That night the six o'clock news had a lot to say about the crash as well as showing some live footage of it. Although preliminary, they said the early indication appeared to have been an explosion from the baggage compartment that caused the crash. The pilot had made radio contact with Pounds Regional Airport in Tyler as he was making his final descent and asked for permission to land when suddenly all communication stopped and the control tower heard what sounded like an explosion.

I didn't get any sleep that night. In fact, I spent a good part of it sitting in the porch swing covered with a wool blanket. This had to have been either Lopez's or Hagan's doings, or perhaps both. Now, what do I do about it, or had I done enough already?

The next morning, I went to the office with Dad and found Albert Jennings parked in front waiting for us. He said he received the message I left yesterday and the agents immediately swarmed the DFW airport, but they saw no sign of Hagen. We all walked into the office together and Dad put on a pot of coffee. Soon, we were discussing the Idaho adventure, and not surprisingly, Albert already knew all about what took place, including my wound. He was surprised to learn from my phone message that Hagen was on the Delta flight to Dallas. He wondered if the agents in Boise were not very efficient and had missed Hagen. He immediately got on the telephone and was instructing someone to review the surveillance video of yesterday morning's passengers departing from Boise to Dallas DFW. He wanted to know if they could see Robert Hagan boarding the plane. If they did, he said he would be very upset that they missed that vital piece of information yesterday. He told them to let him know as soon as they found out about the evidence or lack of it.

I told Albert what Hagan said as he walked by me on the plane and that I have felt very uneasy from that time on. I told him how upset I was that my cell phone was dead and that I had been unable to call him at that time. I also told him I hadn't known whether to alert the flight attendant and take the chance of Hagen killing half the people on the flight, or just keep quiet about it until I reached Dallas. I decided to wait.

I told him that I had a strong inclination that we should not board the plane to Tyler, and then we learned that the plane was blown out of the sky. Surely this was no mere coincidence. I could see wheels starting to turn in Albert's head, and then after a few seconds, he said, "I tend to agree. This does not fit the profile of a middle east terrorist attack, but it does fit the vengeful retaliation of Lopez and Hagan toward you. I believe he was after you. Does Hagan know that you were not on that plane?" Albert asked.

"I don't know. I never saw him again after he boarded the plane in Boise."

"So we really don't know if he got off in Dallas, or if he perhaps, flew on to Atlanta because our agents found no sign on him at the airport in Dallas. However, our surveillance does not show him boarding the plane to Tyler nor getting off in Dallas or in Atlanta. I wonder if he wore some kind of disguise, such as a wig, that would have prevented us from recognizing him?" Albert said.

I told him that it was possible that Hagan slipped out the back door in Boise and never made the flight, but that would have been highly unlikely and unorthodox to have a plane nearing time for takeoff and someone open the emergency backdoor to let a passenger off.

While we were kicking around ideas, Albert received a phone call from his agent in Boise. He told him that it did indeed show Hagan boarding the Delta Flight to Dallas and that they were extremely sorry they had missed that piece of information the day before. They had seen nothing of him since, so who knows where he is now.

Albert suggested that we brainstorm a little. "Let's assume that he thinks you were killed in the plane crash. My guess is that he will head on down to Mexico when this is over. However, I bet he is still somewhere watching until they announce the names of the ones killed in the crash just to make sure that you are dead. When that list is made public, and your name is not on it, then you better keep a watch out".

"Do you think he knows where to find me in East Texas?" I asked.

"You bet! You can count on it." He replied. "So maybe that should be our strategy. Use you as bait, and when he makes his move, we nab him."

Dad was not too keen on that idea as he felt it was too risky for me, but he had nothing better to offer. After a little more talking, Albert said he had some things to check out and instructed me to lay low and not do anything to hurt my side.

After Albert left, Dad said he didn't like the way things were shaping up, and I told him that I didn't either, but what could I do? He said I could go home and try to relax for now and not leave the house or be seen out in public. Then he told me the story about his Uncle Lewis getting crossways with some bad people and how they found him here in East Texas, and one day at Uncle Ben's, they shot and killed Aunt Sara. So it's not too hard for the bad guys to find you here if they want to. The Scroggins name is pretty familiar in these parts and most anyone can tell someone where to find us. "So, Son, stay out of sight for your safety and my peace of mind."

I agreed to do as Dad wished and went back home and finished reading my *Sports Illustrated*. The article said Logan was being suggested by some as a Heisman Trophy candidate which was most unusual for a freshman. I was so proud of him. I decided to call Coach Bevels and let him know that I was hearing great things about Logan and his team, but instead of using my cell phone, I decided I'd use Dad's landline.

Coach Bevels seemed really glad to hear from me, and before hanging up, he asked me if I would be interested in being one of his assistant coaches. He said he was planning to get in touch with me after this year's season was over because his offensive coach told him last week that he was retiring after this season. He said he was wondering and hoping that I would consider taking the job. I told him that I would most certainly think about it.

He then asked me what I'd been doing lately. I told him I had been in Idaho on a hunting trip. I figured that was an honest answer without having to do a lot of explaining. Next, he asked me if I had any luck to which I said, "Some, but the real trophy got away." Then we agreed that sometime after the first of the year, I'd make a trip down there to discuss the coaching position.

That night, when Dad got home, he had some information from Albert that he wanted to share. They had Hagan on camera as being the last passenger to get off the plane in Dallas, but he was wearing a wig which made it very difficult to recognize him. Then they had pictures of him meeting a younger Mexican couple. They were seen leaving the airport together and getting into a blue 2015 Ford Explorer. As the Explorer was driving away from the terminal, they got the license plate number. From there, they traced the Explorer to a Jesse Sanchez of 248 Twelfth Ave in Oak Cliff. Albert said he had a stakeout at the place and that Hagan had been spotted twice inside the house. So for now, we know where he is.

17

Chapter

Imust admit that I felt better knowing that Hagan was under surveillance, but I wondered why he was in Oak Cliff and why he wasn't making a move toward me. I mentioned this to Talisa, and she said she thought that he was just trying to get into my head and cause me mental anguish. I told her if that was what he was trying to do, then he had certainly succeeded because I was about to go crazy worrying and waiting for something to happen. She smiled and gave me a peck on the cheek and said everything was going to be all right and for me to just relax.

"Right. Easy for you to say," I replied with a smile.

The next day, Dad brought me a copy of the *Dallas Morning News* which had front-page coverage of the plane crash. Toward the end of one of the stories, there was a list of names of the ones who were killed. If Hagan saw that, which I'm sure he did, then he must know by now that I was not on the list. I wished somehow the FBI would have embedded my name among the causalities, but they didn't.

Before Dad went back to the office, I asked him, "Now what am I supposed to do? Just sit around and wait for him to pick me off on his own terms like a duck on a pond?"

"Well, I'm not sure, but sitting around until your wound heals is not a bad idea," he said. Then he asked how it was doing, and I told him I couldn't tell that it was much better other than it wasn't bleeding as much.

After everyone had gone to work and I was alone, I started thinking about being the offensive coordinator for the LSU Tigers and Logan. In my mind, I laid out several plays that I thought would really work well for Logan. The more I thought about it, the more excited I became. Finally, I called Coach Bevels on the phone and asked if there was any way we could get together tomorrow. He put me on hold as he looked at his schedule, and after a few seconds, he got back and said that he had a full docket until about five o'clock. I told him that should work perfectly for me, and we agreed to meet at his office at about five.

Later that evening when everyone had gotten home, I ran the idea of going to Louisiana tomorrow by Dad, and he thought it would be a good thing for me mentally as well as for security. "After all, I need to get you off my payroll," he joked. At least I think he was joking. But it would be nice to have a regular paycheck coming in. According to the doctor's orders, I wasn't sure if I should be driving, so Janet insisted Talisa go and drive us to Baton Rouge. I talked with Dad about the plays I had in mind. It was so refreshing to be thinking and talking about something besides Hagan.

The next morning, we got up and off before 9:00 which allowed us time to leisurely make our way across east Texas and the state of Louisiana. We stopped at a couple of out-of-the-way spots that I knew served authentic Cajun food, which I hadn't had in quite some time. We rolled onto the LSU campus about 4:00 and decided to go to the football field and maybe catch the end of their workout. But by the time we got there, the players were heading to the locker room, so we left and drove to the coach's office and waited in the car. We didn't have to wait very long before Coach Bevels arrived and motioned us to get out and come inside. We had a little chit-chat before talking about the job position. Coach said this job would be different from the recruiting job in a lot of ways, and one was the pay structure. He said I would not have an expense account like before but would have a fixed salary with incentive bonuses if the team met different play-off levels. He said the base salary would be $125,000 a year. I thought I had surely misunderstood what he said and asked him to repeat it! I couldn't believe they would pay so much!

He said I would be in the public's eye which could be very good or very cruel. "As you well know, fans will turn on you in a minute. Sometimes they will be cheering you and then booing you in the same game. It's crazy, but that's how they are."

He said I would be expected to implement a game plan that would enhance Logan's abilities, but not exclusively him. He spoke highly of their junior quarterback and said he had an arm like a rocket and could pass with the accuracy of the best of 'em.

"One problem you will have is that six of our offensive linemen will graduate this year. I have asked our recruiters to go after some big, agile linemen. As you well know, without those big men up front, even a Logan can't do very much. So there is the challenge. Are you up to it?" he asked.

"Coach, since we talked on the phone, I have thought of very little else. I think I can do the job. Granted, it's different than what I've done before, but I promise you that no one will put any more effort into the job than I will."

"Richard, I know you will give it your all and never give up. If it was solely up to me to make the decision, I'd hire you today, but I have a board to convince. However, let me say that they have previously pretty much gone with my recommendations, and I certainly plan to recommend you. The drawback might be your lack of experience as a coach."

"When should I know something?" I asked.

"Oh, typically this type of negotiating doesn't take place until after all the bowl games are over, which is sometime in mid-January. But I might be able to convince them to go ahead and make a decision earlier since we already know there is going to be a vacancy. I can try to sell the idea of getting a new coach as soon as possible in order to get an early start on next year's offensive strategy. I expect to have an answer in a few weeks, if not sooner."

When we finished talking, I asked if I could take him and Logan out for a bite to eat. He agreed, and soon the four of us were eating at *Stateline Steakhouse*. When I lived here before, this was one of my favorite places to eat. During our meal, no less than a dozen people stopped by to shake hands with Logan or to get his autograph. He told me that he never envisioned such treatment, but he knew that I did, and for that, he would be forever grateful. It was such a blessing to be talking with him and to see the humble attitude that he maintained. I told him to never get so big that he forgot his roots, and he assured me that he would never let that happen, and I believed him.

Before we left, Coach Bevels did what I was dying to do and that was to tell Logan that I was in line for the offensive coaching position. I wish you could have seen Logan's eyes widen with the news! I believe he was more excited about it than I was. "Mr. Scroggins, I will run my heart out for you; you'll see!"

"Logan, I know you will, but I don't want you to be anything more than yourself. If you just be you, then we will be in good shape."

Finally, the meal was over, and Talisa and I spent the night in a motel by the river. It was a cool night, but beautiful. From our second-floor porch, we could see the Mississippi River and the half-moon hovering over it. She stood in front of me, and I wrapped my arms around her waist as she tilted her head onto my chest and whispered how beautiful the moon was. I agreed and said, "You know the amazing thing is that we are seeing the same moon that Dad and Janet can see and even the same one that Betsy can see in Idaho. We live in a remarkable world."

The next morning, I felt really good about my chances of landing the coaching job, and I told Talisa that $125K wasn't too shabby either. She was already planning on where we might start looking for an apartment, and right in the middle of our conversation, she said, "and we don't want to overlook the church. Richard, it's important that we establish a close church family like what your folks have in East Texas." I agreed with her whole-heartedly and thought it was wonderful for her to mention that.

When we got home, Dad said Albert Jennings was keeping him informed as to Hagan's whereabouts, and it seemed that he was headed back to Mexico. I was shocked and couldn't believe what I was hearing. Apparently, Hagan got wind of the stakeout, but not before the FBI had programmed the Explorer into their satellite tracking database, which meant they could find that car wherever it went, and now it was outside Del Rio.

I told Dad that something was wrong. This just didn't sound right. In fact, it sounded too good to be true, and if it sounds too good, then it probably is. I asked him why they didn't stop and arrest Hagan, and he said he wondered the same thing, but all Albert would say was that they had their reasons.

While we were talking, the telephone rang, and I heard Dad say, "Speaking of the devil. Richard and I were just talking about you." Then I heard silence and Dad was listening very carefully and then said, "Okay, I'll tell him. Thanks for the info and keep us in the loop."

I was eager to hear what Albert said. Dad said they did just what we were talking about. They stopped the Explorer just a few miles from the Texas/Mexico border, and to their surprise, Hagan was not in the car, and they have no idea where or when he got out.

I was really worried now. "It's almost as if he is reading the minds of the FBI and keeping just one step ahead of them." Dad reminded me that Hagan had been in law enforcement for a lot of years. I wondered if Hagan had ever gotten into the car, to begin with. It would have been easy to disguise someone to look like him, and from the distance the agents were watching, they would not be able to tell the difference.

I was uneasy that night and sat up watching television after all the others went to bed. Sometime around midnight, I heard the dogs going off outside. Naturally, I was paranoid and expected Hagan. I got Dad's 357 Magnum out of his gun case and eased out the backdoor for a look. As I eased around, I didn't see anything, but the dogs kept barking. I figured they must have found a skunk or something prowling around. I hoped they would keep their distance if that was indeed why they were barking.

Before going back inside, I decided to check around in front of the house, and as I eased around the corner, I saw the silhouette of someone between the cars and the road. I went a little closer and then yelled out, "Who's there?" As I did, a shot was fired in my direction! I guess they never really saw me and just shot in my general direction. I yelled again for them to drop their gun and come into the light. They shot again, and this time I returned their fire, and I could tell by the moaning sound that I had hit someone. By this time, all the lights were on in the house, and Dad was making his way outside with his shotgun in one hand and a flashlight in the other. I told him that had I hit someone, but we still approached with caution. As we got near the road, I saw the form of a body lying on the ground face down. With guns aimed, we slowly approached, and Dad reached down and rolled him over.

It was Robert Hagan!

"Is he dead?" I asked and Dad said he appeared to be.

We went back into the house and called 911 first and then Albert Jennings. The local sheriff's officers were soon there and confirmed the body was dead, and then they took a report from me. Nothing was disturbed until the justice of the peace arrived and legally pronounced Hagan dead. After a few hours of interrogation and explaining, Albert Jennings arrived. He came into the house and Janet poured him a cup of coffee. By this time, the body had been removed and taken to the local funeral home, but Dad and I both assured Albert that it was Hagan, but for some reason, he still had his doubts. He kept saying that this didn't seem like Hagan's style, and why was he here spying on us in the middle of the night?

I said we didn't know that he was spying in the middle of the night. He may have been here since early afternoon and was trying to leave and that's when the dogs started barking. It probably looked to him as though everyone had gone to bed and that it was time to leave.

Albert agreed that made some sense, "But regardless, Richard, it seems your worries are over, and you can now get on with your life again."

I concurred that it was good that this ordeal was finally over. I hated that so many innocent people were hurt along the way, starting with Agent Taylor losing his life back in the swamp. "But you know, in a way, I feel sorry for Hagan. I wonder if he has any family who cares about him."

"Our records do not show a single relative anywhere. He was a loner that was all by himself."

None of us even went to bed, as it was about five o'clock before the last of the people left. Talisa kept holding to my hand or arm in an attempt to keep me calm. While never voicing it out loud, my inward thoughts were, "I finally got you! You finally got what you deserved, and I was the one that gave it to you." I knew I needed to vent the bitterness I had toward him, but for now, I kept it bottled up inside of me.

Later in the morning, everybody headed to the office and Talisa rode with Janet. I wanted to be alone for a while and promised to be along soon. While everything was finally quiet, I sat at the kitchen table drinking a cup of hot black coffee reliving the events of the night as I looked out the living room window toward the road. In my mind, I could hear the gunshots and see the image in the darkness. I could hear the thud after my shot then the familiar look on Hagan's face when Dad turned him over. I wondered if I'd ever get those images erased from my mind. I supposed only time will tell.

I finished my coffee and got ready to join the others at the office. I really needed this time alone. Before I left, I prayed to God in heaven to help me in adjusting and for forgiveness for taking another man's life.

I got into my car, and as soon as I turned the key, everything exploded, and the entire world was one ball of fire. I felt myself being propelled into the air before hitting something hard. My body felt numb yet warm all over. Everything seemed to be moving in slow motion. I couldn't move anything but my eyes, and they were getting heavy. In the far distance, it seemed I could hear someone saying, "Hey Buddy, don't leave me now. Hang in there. We'll have you to the ER soon. Don't leave me now!"

Vaguely, I could hear sirens and realized I was in an ambulance. Hagan had planted a bomb in my car! I couldn't let him beat me now, but I wasn't sure I could hang on. Could Logan make it without me? What would Talisa do if I leave? I can't die, not just yet.

I must have passed out. The next thing I remember was being on what I guessed to be an operating table. Bright lights were shining in my eyes, and someone said, "He's waking up." Then everything went black.

After that, I remembered hearing people talk, but I couldn't see them nor could I talk to them. I didn't recognize any of the voices and they were talking about blood pressure, pulse rate, etc. I felt pain all over. Then I heard Talisa's voice as she said, "How is he, Doc?"

A man replied, "Not good. He is burned over 90 percent of his body and his vital signs are barely functioning. It will be a miracle if he makes it."

"I will make it. I will NEVER GIVE UP," I thought to myself. I wished I could tell Talisa not to give up on me and that I would be back. We have yet to live our lives together." Then, I heard the frantic sounds of men and women as my mind began to darken.

Epilogue

The funeral for Richard was conducted the day before Thanksgiving. Thanksgiving had always been such a special time for the Scroggins Family, but this year it was different, and their lives would never be the same again.

Logan Pointe sustained a career-ending injury the second game of the following season and never had the opportunity to become the national icon that Richard had envisioned.

Talisa moved back to Houston in an attempt to rebuild her life. Not long after Richard's death, she found out that she was pregnant and gave birth to a baby girl. She named her Hailey because she was conceived in Hailey, Idaho.

Robert and Janet continued running the detective agency, and over the course of time, they adjusted and had some normalcy to their life.

Cap-a-tan Lopez was never heard of again by the Scroggins Family.

Although only twenty-nine years of age, Richard Scroggins made more of an impact on his world than most people do in a life span twice as long as his. His "never give up" attitude touched the lives of so many in a very positive way.

He will forever be remembered.

www.ingramcontent.com/pod-product-compliance
Lightning Source LLC
Chambersburg PA
CBHW071823190726
48292CB00005B/1587